MW00877490

The Destiny of Sunshine Ranch

T.M. GAOUETTE

This book is a work of fiction. Names, characters, places, and incidents are products of the author's imagination or are used fictitiously. Any resemblance to actual events or locales or persons, living or dead, is entirely incidental.

All rights reserved, including the right to reproduce this book or portions thereof in any form whatsoever.

First Edition

Cover designed by T.M. Gaouette

Visit tmgaouette.com for more title and author information

Manufactured in the United States of America

Copyright © 2012 T.M. GAOUETTE

ISBN-13: 978-1470011024
ISBN-10: 1470011026

To God. To my husband.
To my children. To my Godsons.

*"I know both how to be abased, and I know how to abound: every where
and in all things I am instructed both to be full and to be hungry,
both to abound and to suffer need.
I can do all things through Christ which strengtheneth me."*
Philippians 4:12-13

1

THE TIRES CRUNCHED slowly into the sand and came to a halt. The man behind the wheel of the red Ford truck peered out of the open window to gaze on a memory that sat quietly at the base of the rich green, grassy hill. The sun shone over a white farmhouse, comfortably nestled inside the ranch. To its left was a red barn, smaller than he remembered. A paddock enclosed with white post and board fencing sat in front. The dirt road on which he'd stopped meandered down the right side of the aged property, appearing and disappearing through the lush, green trees. Nothing had really changed, it seemed, although no one lived within its boundaries any longer, and both time and neglect had left their weary mark.

The man turned the engine off and leaned his head back against the seat. He continued to survey the property and its surroundings, looking for reminders of his past. The crooked old oak by the house looked even older, as if holding itself up was getting harder day by day. He searched within its leaves and branches, but couldn't see what he was looking for from that distance. The fields were overgrown with wild grass and flowers. He scanned the property with stinging eyes. It all seemed to be there, but only as a scene lost in time, once loved and warmed from within by so many. It was all there, yet so much was missing. A part of him wanted to sit for a while and just take it all in. The other part was eager to drive down to the house and bask in the memories. He stopped himself from breaking into the scene too soon and closed his eyes. His mind took him back to a memory he would have rather forgotten, had it not eventually taken him to a better place.

***

"I'M SORRY to have to call you in again, Miss Ratchet, but we just can't go on like this. I'm afraid we'll have to suspend him again." The school principal sat behind her desk wearing a brown suit and a drained expression.

"Is that really necessary, Miss Martindale?" Denise Ratchet asked, even though she had known this was coming when she'd received the call that morning. She had to admit that caring for these children was not as easy as she'd originally anticipated. Her plan had been to have more.

"We cannot have the distraction. He fights with *everyone.*"

She leaned forward in her chair. "Well, what do you propose I do with him during the day?"

"I'm sorry." Miss Martindale collected her papers and straightened them with a sigh. "Maybe it would be best to meet with his case worker, or contact the state department and see if they can help you. I have a school to run, and I cannot do that when your son—"

"*Foster* son."

"Foster son . . . excuse me . . . continues to cause havoc like he does. You know, he's going to have to repeat the fourth grade at this rate."

"Well, that's just *great.* Thanks for *nothing.*" She got up.

***

Out in the hall, a young boy sat with his head hung low, dark greasy hair falling over his face. He picked at a thread hanging from a hole in the right knee of his pants and yanked until it came off. Then he twisted the piece around his forefinger and watched the tip swell and redden. He knew he was in trouble, but his fear was weakened with lack of concern.

"Come on, you." Miss Ratchet marched toward him and pulled him up by the shoulder of his dirty denim jacket, then shoved him ahead of her.

In the car, she lit a cigarette and sucked in a long drag. Benedict faced forward in silence while, in his peripheral view, he could see her throw him angry glances every few seconds.

"When are you going to stop embarrassing me?"

She waited, taking puffs from the remainder of her cigarette and shoving the butt into an overfilled ashtray. She grabbed her pack of cigarettes and lit another one.

"If you want to get moved on, that's fine with me. I tell you something, I can get the same from any other kid." She turned the wheel, shaking her head. "You all pay out the same."

Benedict wondered if she was still talking to him or to herself again.

"But I wouldn't have to deal with this aggravation."

He said nothing.

"You want to be on the streets?" When he didn't respond, she reached over and whacked him on the forehead, the cigarette clenched between her lips. "Hey, wake up, I'm talking to you."

He looked at her, feeling the sting of her hand.

"Do you want to go live on the streets?"

"No, ma'am."

"Well, then you better get your act together."

A tear rolled down his cheek, and he wiped it away quickly, reprimanding himself for allowing that to happen in front of the woman he hated most in the world.

"Oh, please," she scoffed. "Don't give me that. You think you have it so bad, you have no idea. My mother used to keep a stick, and she wasn't afraid to use it—or whatever else she could get her hands on—so don't you cry about a little tap." She sucked on the cigarette, and for the next few blocks, that was all he had to listen to.

At a stop sign, he watched a woman pushing her toddler in a stroller. The child was holding a lollypop and swinging his legs back and forth. The mother cooed down at him every now and then. *What a crock*, he thought to himself.

"Don't forget who's coming tonight." Miss Ratchet blew the smoke out in his direction. He tried to cover his nose discreetly and opened his window.

"Do you mind? It's freezing out there." She closed his window and locked the access. "You kids better be on your best behavior tonight or you'll be sorry."

She turned into an apartment complex.

"When you get inside, I want you to get that bathroom cleaned up."

In the hallway of her dark apartment, Miss Ratchet threw her keys on a table cluttered with unopened mail and old newspapers.

"Daniel!" She kicked off her shoes. "You get Mel like I told you?"

"Yes, ma'am," Daniel called from another room.

Melanie came running to them. She grabbed Benedict's leg and giggled up at him. He looked down at her expressionless.

"You finish them dishes?" the woman shouted out again.

"Doing them now."

"Benny home, Benny home," the little girl sang her chant.

"*You* . . . go get that bathroom cleaned, and when you're done with that, give these carpets a once-over." She walked into the living room and threw herself into an oversized brown arm chair and lit another cigarette.

"Get off." Benedict wiggled his leg gently and unclenched Melanie's fingers from his pant leg. He headed into the kitchen where Daniel, an older boy, was drying dishes with a discolored yellow towel. Without speaking, Benedict grabbed a plastic cup and poured some water from the faucet. He noticed that the counters had been cleared off, as was protocol for the visit. Gone were the unwashed dishes, filled ashtrays, the mix of cleaned and dirty laundry, and Melanie's soiled pull-ups.

"You know, when you make her mad, she takes it out on all of us." Daniel spoke without looking at him. His greasy blond hair was tucked carelessly behind his ears, revealing the remnants of a four-day-old bruise that stained his left eye.

Benedict looked down at Melanie, who'd followed him into the kitchen. The thought of Miss Ratchet taking anything out on a toddler made his insides burn and his heart beat faster.

They were quiet for a moment as they listened to the woman coughing uncontrollably in the next room. Then she shouted, "Daniel, where's the family picture?"

"I'll get it," he yelled back. He shook his head and threw the towel on the counter. "I can only take so much," he muttered before disappearing out of the kitchen.

He returned with the image of the three children surrounding Miss Ratchet. Benedict watched as Daniel wiped the glass. *It's the perfect show picture.* The boys were dressed in matching green sweaters and Melanie in a jade dress. Miss Ratchet wore an olive blouse. The two boys stared at the picture, and Benedict wondered how many times he'd have to look at it.

He left the kitchen with Melanie running after him. It took him half an hour to clean the bathroom. Miss Ratchet barked her demands from the comfort of her armchair.

"You clean up and around that toilet, you hear me in there? Make sure you scrub that floor."

Her instructions were accompanied by eruptions of coughs. Melanie sat close by, dropping an orange plastic ball into Benedict's empty water cup and tipping it out repeatedly.

"You boys better hurry. You need to clean up too."

"Y'know, if they take you away, you'll probably all end up in prison, because I'm the *only* one who'll put up with you," Miss Ratchet told them, once the housework was done and they'd washed up and changed.

They sat side by side on the couch in order of height, just as she liked it. The scent of a cheap vanilla candle wafted through the air and mixed in with the musty stink of old cigarettes.

"I want you all to realize just how lucky you are to have a roof over your heads." She nodded over at them and Melanie squirmed next to Benedict. "It ain't fun out there in the big world, so don't think you can do better anywhere else. I've seen other homes. I know what a bad home's like."

She nodded again, her eyes wide as she glanced from one child to another. Melanie grabbed Benedict's hand and he pulled it away. Miss Ratchet puffed on her cigarette.

"So you better be on your best behavior."

When the doorbell rang, she gave them a warning look before standing up. She straightened Melanie's dress, checked the boys' attire, and tapped the foundation around Daniel's eye.

Benedict wished he could wear clean jeans every day.

"Prison," she whispered, adding, "smile," in her fake cheery, *I'm a great loving foster parent* voice. She put her cigarette out and walked to the door.

This time, the visitor was a man none of the children knew. Even though he was tall and lanky and looked like he'd just graduated from college, Miss Ratchet fluttered her overly made-up eyes at him and played her part well. The children just sat and smiled, nodding when appropriate. The visit didn't take long. It never did.

"Well, everything seems to be in order, Miss Ratchet." The man gulped down the rest of his now cold coffee and smiled. "As you know, we appreciate folks like you."

"I like to do my part." Miss Ratchet cocked her head to one side and pressed her lips together. "It takes a village, right?"

"That's what most people don't get." He looked thoughtful. "But you do, and that's what we need more of, women like you who open up your homes and offer the most selfless of gifts—your love and attention. We *thank* you for that."

Benedict wanted to cry out that it was all a scam, but he knew that the man wouldn't believe him and that they'd all suffer the consequences when he left. So he sat quietly.

"Ok, so . . ." The man put on his jacket. "Same time next—"

Something on the bookshelf next to Miss Ratchet caught his attention. He walked slowly toward it while she watched, biting her lip. He picked up the green family picture and smiled.

"Look at that." He shook his head. "I love it when a family comes together."

He was about to place the picture back on the bookshelf when he was distracted by something tucked in between two books. He reached in and pulled out a plastic bag filled with a dried herb substance, a couple of handmade cigarettes, and another bag with white powder.

Benedict wasn't sure why the man's soft smile became tight-lipped in a second. He scowled at Miss Ratchet with eyes narrowed in accusation. Benedict heard Daniel scoff slightly. Miss Ratchet stood up quickly, her mouth and eyes opened wide, but no sound came from her.

The man pointed at her. "You will remain seated if you don't mind." He pulled out a cell phone from his jacket pocket and dialed. Benedict noticed his hands were shaking.

Miss Ratchet slumped back into her chair, biting her nails nervously. At that moment, things seemed to speed up.

Suddenly, she started to cry and shake her head. She kept repeating, "It's not mine, it's not mine."

But the man wasn't listening because he was giving their address to the person on the phone. He snapped the phone shut and stared at Miss Ratchet without saying a word. When she began to protest again, he shook his head and put his hand up, saying, "Save it for the authorities, ma'am."

Nothing else was said at that point. Miss Ratchet sobbed, and the children glanced from her to each other and then to the man who now wore a frown, as if betrayed by the love of his life.

Almost half an hour of awkwardness passed before another man, with black rimmed glasses, and a young redheaded woman walked into the room. The three talked together, gesturing to the children, until the woman nodded and approached them.

"You guys need to get some overnight stuff together.

Don't be scared, okay?"

She reached out to touch Melanie's cheek. The child leaned against Benedict.

Daniel didn't look scared. In fact, Benedict could swear that he caught him smirking every now and then. He wasn't scared either. He'd been through this over and over again. What was another house? Melanie was scared, though. He could tell by the way she clutched his hand. This time he let her.

The drive to the next home wasn't long. "It's just for the night," the woman with the red hair had said before leaving them. "We'll be back in the morning to reassign you."

The mother at this house said very little to them once she supplied blankets and pillows. None of the children wanted anything to eat, so she nodded, smiled nervously, and put out the light.

"Great, just what we need." Daniel lay on his back and looked up at the ceiling fan while they listened to Melanie's quiet snoring. She'd fallen asleep curled up on the couch behind them. "I'm eighteen next year, you know." He looked over at Benedict. "I don't need to put up with this anymore."

***

IN THE MORNING, Daniel was gone. The police were called, but Benedict and Melanie didn't get to see him again or know what ever became of him. Instead, they were taken in a car to an office building in the city, where they sat side by side in a reception area.

Melanie held Benedict's hand while they watched in a room with glass walls while the red-haired woman talked to another woman, introduced to them as Miss Davis. Miss Davis sat behind a desk covered with two messy heaps of files and scattered documents and, as the women talked, she smiled, nodded, and occasionally flipped through files. She was on the phone part of the time and occasionally glanced over at the two children, until finally she got up and headed toward them.

"Come with me, Melanie." Miss Davis bent toward the little girl and held her hand out. But Melanie pushed in closer against Benedict and turned her head to hide her face.

Benedict just watched Miss Davis. He could feel the little girl press harder into his side.

"I have something to show you." Miss Davis signaled to another woman who disappeared and then, moments later, returned with a worn out Raggedy Ann doll. "Look." Miss Davis held it out to the girl.

Melanie turned her head so one eye peeked out. Seeing the doll, she reached out for it, loosening her grip on Benedict's arm. Once the doll was in her hand, Miss Davis leaned in and picked her up.

As if suddenly realizing that she'd been duped, Melanie began screaming and kicking and flailing her arms. She dropped the doll and reached out to Benedict with both arms. He watched silently, trying not to let her anguish-filled face affect him. He swallowed hard and felt a lump stuck in his throat.

"Benny, no . . . no . . . no . . . me want Benny . . . Benny!"

The girl's high-pitched scream turned the heads of everyone on the floor. They had probably all seen similar scenes in the past, but it still visibly pained them to watch.

Miss Davis couldn't hold the child as she fought to escape, and when she put her down, Melanie ran to Benedict and clung to his leg.

"Benedict, you need to let her go," Miss Davis told him

sternly.

Benedict lifted both his hands, shrugged, and raised his eyebrows. "I'm not holding her."

Melanie sobbed hysterically, choking and gagging on her own spit. "Me want Benny. Me want Benny."

Miss Davis looked around and saw a gathering of associates standing and waiting for her to make her next move. She scratched her head.

"Okay, I have an idea." She went back into the glass room.

Benedict reached down and grabbed Melanie's hand, and the little girl climbed onto his lap. He didn't object, but instead put his arms around her, because he felt she needed it and he needed it, too. It was a strange sensation, having someone cling to him so desperately, looking to him for protection.

They all watched and waited as Miss Davis made another phone call. Before long she returned.

"Okay, that's settled," she said, satisfied. "You two can stay together and we've found the perfect place."

Yeah right, Benedict thought. *Where have I heard that before?*

2

THE JOURNEY to the new home was a long one that took them a few hours, through the city and into the suburbs. Benedict watched as the scenery gradually changed from tall, brick structures and dirty, slushy streets to backed-up highways, then again into long, winding roads with nothing but an abundance of bare winter trees lining embankments, still covered in snow.

They arrived late that night, and although he had tried to stay awake, he and Melanie both fell asleep. He barely remembered meeting the new foster mother, but did recall that this time there was also a foster father, David, in the house. He'd never had one before. Miss Davis and the parents talked briefly before Martha, the foster mother, led Benedict and Melanie to their rooms.

He woke right before sunrise and lay for a few minutes before he realized that something heavy was on his feet. It was Melanie, curled up asleep on the end of his bed.

He lay back and looked at the ceiling. The house smelled different. He wasn't sure of what, but it was different from all the other places he'd stayed at. He knew for sure what it didn't smell of though: cigarettes and dirty diapers.

He pulled his feet gently from under Melanie and turned to look around the room. There was a small bookcase on the right side of his bed, with more books lining the shelves than he'd seen in his lifetime. He tried to read some of the titles, but it was too dark in the room. There was also a dresser against the wall opposite him, with a large picture hanging above. It showed wild horses galloping in a field. A bedside table with a yellow lamp was to his left. And on the wall above his head, hung a picture of the Virgin Mary cradling her baby Jesus. Benedict sat up and turned to get a better look at that picture. He wondered if his own mother, whoever she was, had ever held him the same way. *Yeah, right. A mother who held her baby that way would never let go.*

He got out of bed, walked over to the window, and peeked out. The sun was coming up and he could see some of the land around the home. Large patches of snow splattered the ground like islands floating in an ocean of flattened, brown grass. His new home was set on a farm. *That's a first.*

Melanie stirred and sat up, rubbing her eyes and watching him quietly. He went to the door, opened it slowly, and peeked out into the dark hallway. Melanie climbed off the bed and followed him. As they made their way down the stairs, he noticed a plaque hanging on the wall that read, "I can do all things through Christ, which strengtheneth me." *Great! Another nut house.*

Melanie followed him into the kitchen. He wasn't used to everything being so neat and tidy. He stood for a moment, scanning the clean granite countertops and herbs growing on the window shelf, to the oversized wooden dining table with a large bowl of apples and bananas.

The fridge door was covered with photographs. He walked over to get a closer look. One picture showed two children chasing another with a water pistol. Another showed children sitting on a deck eating a pie of some kind. There were also pictures of David and Martha hugging some kids, eating with others, and riding horses. *Show pictures,* Benedict concluded as he opened the fridge door and thought of Miss Ratchet. He looked in the fridge and his mouth opened when he saw the shelves filled. *It's like a grocery store.* He reached for the milk.

When he closed the fridge, the kitchen door opened and an old man walked in, wearing a worn out, wide-brimmed straw hat and distressed work clothes. At first, the man didn't see them, and Benedict considered hiding. Melanie clutched his leg just as the man flicked on the light, looked over at them, and gasped in surprise.

"Thought I was the only one up," the man said, grinning. He pulled his hat off, revealing greasy straggles of gray hair, and nodded toward them. "Good morning."

Benedict didn't respond. Melanie peeked up at the man from behind Benedict's leg.

"Abraham Jones." He reached out his hand, but Benedict didn't take it. "I help out the Credence family here at Sunshine Ranch, off and on."

The man pulled his hand back, smiled, walked past the children, and began making some coffee.

"So you two must be new." Mr. Jones glanced down at Melanie. "Hey, little lady."

She pulled back a bit, but reappeared with a slight smile and a gleam in her eye. Benedict wasn't afraid either.

Mr. Jones gathered five coffee cups on the counter and reached his hand out to Benedict. "May I?"

Benedict looked down and realized that he was still holding the milk, so he handed it over, just as David walked into the kitchen from upstairs.

"Ahh, good morning!" David threw his hands up when

he saw the children.

Benedict thought that the man seemed too cheerful for so early in the morning, but he could also tell that he wasn't faking it.

"And Melanie." He bent down toward her. "How are you this lovely morning?" She said nothing. "You guys are up early. Does that mean you're going to help Mr. Jones and me with the horses? We have a new one arriving this morning."

"No, it does *not*." It was the foster mother this time. She appeared from behind her husband, and Benedict wondered why she was so happy. "I hope you two slept well."

She came over to them and reached her arms out, but Benedict backed up surprised.

She stopped suddenly. "I'm sorry."

"Martha has a tendency to hug, kiss, and squish every child she meets," David said.

Mr. Jones handed her a cup and chuckled.

"Oh, David." She looked back at them crinkling her nose, but then laughed. "Okay, he's right, I do." She took a sip of coffee and set her cup on the counter before pulling out a bowl of eggs and some bacon from the fridge. "Anyway, we are a family of pancake lovers," she began. "I hope you two are also—"

"Pancakes," came a little voice from behind Benedict's legs.

Martha looked down at Melanie with a grin. "You like pancakes?" Martha kneeled down in front of the child. Melanie nodded and smiled.

"Great." Martha said. "Maybe you can help me make them?" She extended her arms again, but cautiously, and this time the little girl came out from behind Benedict and allowed Martha to pick her up.

"You know, we have some serious pancake making to do." She plopped the little girl on the counter and set a bowl and bag of flour next to her.

"Yes, you do," David said. "And we have some serious horse poop to muck up." He reached out and ruffled Benedict's hair as he made his way out the kitchen door with Mr. Jones behind him, but not before asking, "You sure you don't want to help?"

This time Benedict smiled.

"You should eat before the others wake up." Martha smiled and pointed to Benedict's plate with her fork. "You don't want to fight for your first meal here."

Benedict didn't know what she meant by that, so he continued to eat slowly while he watched Melanie climb onto Martha's lap. He felt a little sad, but ignored the feeling. He was tired of her climbing all over him, anyway.

"Oh, you're a cuddle bunny." Martha welcomed the child into her arms. "I like that."

As she talked to Benedict now, she looked into his eyes, and it made him a little uncomfortable.

"I knew I smelled pancakes." A tall blond girl walked into the kitchen and came up behind Martha. She kissed her cheek and Martha hugged her with her free arm.

"Good morning, Eva," Martha said and added, "Please meet Benedict and Melanie." She gestured toward Benedict who was now looking at the table. "Benedict, this is Eva."

The girl smiled and waved, just as a tall teenage boy rushed past her, running his fingers through his sandy hair. "Oh . . . and Sebastian."

Sebastian raised his hand in greeting and then asked, "Is David outside yet?" He kissed Martha before he added, "I think the new gelding is here."

Then he noticed Melanie curled on Martha's lap and winked at her. "Hey, little one."

Melanie pulled back into Martha, but her eyes sparkled and she smiled shyly.

"He sure is," Martha said and the boy headed for the door. "Wait, Sabe. Eat something first."

The boy turned and grabbed a pancake. After smothering it in butter and syrup and folding it in half, he took a huge bite. Martha shook her head as he grabbed a waiting coffee and winked at her before leaving the kitchen.

"Wise guy," she muttered with a grin.

Eva helped herself to breakfast and joined them at the table.

Benedict noticed Melanie was playing with Martha's necklace, her little head resting against her. "I'm going to get dressed." He stood up, feeling uneasy sitting in his pajamas with strangers.

Martha smiled and Melanie sat up straight, her eyes wide in fear.

"I'll be back," he said in a softer voice.

"Oh, Benedict?" Martha called after him. He turned to look at her. "I teach school here at home. You don't have to start today, but after the weekend, I'd like to begin working with you, okay?"

He hadn't heard of anything like teaching at home, so he just nodded and turned away.

"Oh, and Benedict?"

He waited, not turning this time.

"I'm really happy you and Melanie are here."

3

AS BENEDICT climbed the stairs toward the bedroom, another girl came rushing down. She didn't seem to notice him at first and nearly knocked him over, but she lifted her head just in time to see him. She stopped abruptly. Her long black hair had fading red streaks and was still tousled from sleep, but she'd made up her face with black eyeliner and lipstick. Her nose was pierced with a tiny diamond stud that Benedict had a hard time not staring at.

"Hey." She squinted at him in confusion. "You new?"

Benedict muttered, "Yes."

She responded with a smile and a nod before pushing her hand toward him. "Cool. I'm Tommie by the way."

"Benedict."

"Good." Continuing down the stairs at a slower pace, she added, "Welcome to the nut house."

Back in the bedroom, he dressed in the jeans he had worn the day before and a yellow t-shirt, crumpled from a rushed packing job. He then emptied all his clothes onto the floor and began rolling each item before packing it back into his bag. Once done, he put the bag in the back of the empty closet.

At that moment, shouts resonated from outside—one was in the distance, and one nearby. He peered out of the window to see what the commotion was, absently trying to flatten the creases in his shirt.

Sebastian was standing near the house below him, looking out toward the fields, beyond the paddock where David was signaling to him. Sebastian seemed to understand the message, nodded, and walked toward the house.

The sun was brightening the day and melting a winter that had far overstayed its welcome, and Benedict had a sudden urge to go outside. He grabbed his jacket and descended the stairs quietly, so he could escape without being bothered.

While the rest of the kids were in class, Benedict explored. He stood on the porch first, where five white wooden rocking chairs lined the walls. Their pristine appearance contrasted with the fading paint of the porch. In some areas, the paint was peeling and the wood beneath splintered. But the red hanging plants were lush and vibrant, advertising the love and devotion they received from someone who cared.

Some of the boards creaked slightly as he walked. He glanced up the road they'd driven down the night before, rocking back and forth on the broken bottom step. The sun warmed his face, while a cold wind chilled his body. He felt a happiness that he couldn't ever remember feeling before.

He put on his jacket and zipped it up, telling himself to cut it out. *This isn't real life.* But his thoughts were cut off when the sound of flapping caught his attention. He looked up at the large flag above his head, worn at the edges by the unmerciful seasons of New England. It extended from the end of a tarnished metal pole attached to the porch roof. He imagined it'd keep on flying until it no longer could.

Benedict strolled slowly around the right side of the house, and the uneven ground squelched under each step. He bowed his head under dormant crab-apple trees, and jumped over muddy puddles and patches of snow. To his left, he saw three horses in a large paddock. Mr. Jones was bending over some project outside the front of the large red barn.

Just as he neared the back of the house, Benedict heard screaming coming from inside.

"Benny, Benny, me want Benny!"

Recognizing the little voice and his name, his heart jumped and he rushed for the doorway inside, but it opened before he reached it.

A heavy-set, older woman, wearing a long cream apron, stepped out. She smiled cheerfully, although somewhat frazzled, and before she could say anything, little Melanie stumbled past her toward him. She reached her arms around him and buried her wet face against him. He tried to pry her off him, but she held on tight and cried hard.

"She just woke up from a quick nap. Everything's still strange to her . . . I'm Nana Credence, David's mother. You must be little Benedict." The woman extended her hand for him to shake. "Are you okay?"

He nodded but didn't say anything.

"Well, we're happy to have you. Oh, and David's heading into town after Martha's finished teaching, and he can usually be persuaded to take along some kids." She lifted her eyebrows playfully and grinned. "You okay with Mel?" She looked at the little girl who sobbed softly.

He nodded and she smiled before disappearing inside. Her words *happy to have you* played over and over in his head and he wondered how long that sentiment would last.

He felt Melanie's hand slide into his, and he held it loosely. She skipped awkwardly as they walked, her mood suddenly brighter. Probably a result of the sunny day and the closeness of the only family she had, he presumed, since he felt it, too. They walked around the whole house until they returned to the front porch, where he sat down on a step. Melanie sat next to him.

"Don't get too comfortable," Benedict said to the little girl as she leaned on him. "This is just another stop, and then we'll be moved on again."

Melanie didn't respond or even look like she was listening to him. She just gazed out into the distance, a soft smile resting on her lips as he spoke.

He picked at the peeling paint between his feet. "It's nice and all, it all looks good, but it's not real. So, don't you get all attached." He looked down at her. She continued to stare out into nothing, as if entranced. "The truth will come out, you wait and see."

"What are you talking about?" a voice said from behind them and he turned abruptly.

Melanie's head fell onto his lap. She sat up and would have cried, but she was clearly as curious as he was about the young girl standing in the doorway of the house behind the screen door. Benedict didn't say anything.

"I'm Isabella. I'm seven." The girl pushed the screen door open and made her way down the steps, so that she stood in front of them. She smiled at Melanie, but the little girl just hid her face in her usual shy manner.

"She doesn't like anyone but me," Benedict said and Isabella frowned. He didn't care that he sounded mean. He was feeling mean and all he wanted was to be left alone. But by the looks of it, no one could be alone at this house. "How many kids live here, anyway?" He tried to sound like the answer really didn't matter.

"Well, there's me, Eva . . ." She counted on her fingers. "Tommie, Sebastian is the oldest, he's seventeen, we call him Sabe, um . . . and little Francine . . . she came all the way from China, y'know."

Benedict didn't know that and he didn't care. He also didn't know how one family could have so many kids. It was then that he decided that not getting attached would definitely be the smartest approach.

"The others are still in school, but I'm all done. I'm always done first." Isabella crushed snow with her toes before settling next to them.

***

BENEDICT DIDN'T have to beg to be taken into town like the others. David said he got first dibs, just for being new. Sebastian, Eva, and Tommy also got picked, but Benedict didn't see how they couldn't have been, since no one else wanted to go and the truck had room for all of them. Isabella wanted to stay and play school with Melanie and Francine, who was about the same age. And Benedict was a little hurt that the little girl didn't seem to notice that he was leaving.

Bates Tackle & More was the destination, and as David filled his basket with fishing and hunting supplies, Benedict walked the aisles and scanned the endless shelves. There were fishing reels and poles, tackles, lures, ammunition, cleaning kits, and a multitude of other items he couldn't identify.

He noticed Eva and Tommie whispering and giggling together. Sebastian walked past them and shook his head, as if he knew what their scheme entailed.

"David." The girls sang his name as they rushed either side of him and hooked their arms into his.

"Oh, here it comes." David spoke in a low voice,

without looking up from the box of fishing flies that he was reading.

"Pleeeease?"

"Go on then, I'll meet you there."

The girls whispered, "Yes" in unison.

With his eyes still on the box, David pulled his wallet from his back pocket and handed it to Eva who took out some cash and handed it back.

"Come on," Tommie said to Benedict.

Partly out of boredom and partly out of curiosity, he followed them out of the store. As they walked a couple of blocks, Benedict was fascinated by the quaint little shops and the bank that looked like a regular house. The characteristics of the small town were very different from those of the big city.

They crossed the road and Tommie said, "Miss Milly's lemon meringue pies are *amazing*."

A tiny bell announced their entrance, and Benedict scanned the café in wonder. There were about eight tables in the room, and each was covered with a red and white checkered tablecloth, topped with a small glass vase holding a single white daisy. At the far end was a breakfast bar where two men sat eating with their backs to them. There were about seven customers scattered among the tables.

The children walked toward the counter and, as they passed two young teenage boys sitting at a table, Tommie offered a short wave to one of the boys. Both she and Eva said, "Hey, Faden," at the same time. The dark haired boy looked embarrassed, but he also raised his hand, smiled, and then looked down at his plate. Benedict noticed the other boy glare at Faden.

"That's Faden," Eva said. "He's David's ranch hand. He's really cool."

"His brother, on the other hand . . ." Tommie

whispered. Eva nudged her and threw her a warning look.

After paying for their pies, Eva headed toward the door, and again, while passing the boys, Tommie said, "See you later?"

Faden looked up, but before he could answer, the other boy sighed.

"Do you mind?" Some of the other customers looked over. "My brother and I are trying to eat here."

"Roy," Faden said, but the older boy stared back at him defiantly and he fell silent, returning his eyes to his plate.

Under Roy's glare, Tommie's cheeks reddened and her eyes glistened as she rushed out the door. Benedict and Eva followed quickly.

"Don't worry about it," Eva said kindly, but Tommie said nothing and Benedict followed quietly.

"Hey!" a voice called out. They turned around to see Roy, with Faden following behind him, apparently protesting his brother's intentions.

"This is your last warning. I don't want you talking to my brother in public. I don't care if he works for David Credence. He doesn't work for you rejects, okay?"

"Cut it out, Roy." Faden's face was flushed with anger.

Roy turned to his brother and whacked him on the back of the head and then proceeded toward the girls and Benedict. "Who's that?" He pointed at Benedict.

"Mind your own business." Tommie's defiance crumbled a little as her bottom lip trembled. Eva nudged her, but she stood her ground. "You don't scare me, Roy."

"I'm not trying to scare you, reject."

"Don't call her that," Faden said.

Roy looked back at his brother. "You need to shut it. I'm trying to talk to these rejects."

He turned back to Tommie and they stood almost face to face now.

"Look at you, with your freaky hair and makeup. You look like a clown." He started laughing.

Benedict couldn't stand the sound, or the way that Faden, Tommie, and Eva all seemed to be afraid of this boy. He wasn't afraid—he had dealt with boys like this all his life. In fact, he'd dealt with worse, and he wasn't afraid any more.

Without thinking, he pushed past the girls and threw himself against Roy's chest. The boy was visibly caught off guard and he took a few steps back to regain his balance, but Benedict wasn't strong enough to knock him to the ground.

Roy's face turned red. He tightened his lips and threw his arms into Benedict's shoulders, knocking him fiercely to the ground. The girls rushed to his aid and Faden pulled his brother back. Benedict scrambled to get up, but he wasn't quick enough. Roy managed to pull away from his brother's grip and threw himself on top of Benedict before he could get to his feet. Roy's punch swiped the side of his mouth, and the girls screamed.

A loud *Hey* bellowed over them.

Benedict felt the weight of Roy's body lift off his. He gazed up, stunned to find Sebastian looking down at Roy.

"Get your hands off him," Sebastian shouted, his face twisted in anger. "Don't you touch him again, Roy Simms. Don't you touch anyone in my family."

Roy got to his feet shakily, slowly backing away from Sebastian whose eyes flashed with the passion of a wolf.

"Family?" he scoffed. "None of you are even Credences." He began running up the road yelling, "You're just a bunch of rejects," leaving Faden standing alone.

Sebastian helped Benedict to his feet and looked at his face. "What's going on?" He spoke through gritted teeth.

Benedict saw pain behind the anger in the boy's eyes.

He'd seen it many times before in the mirror.

"I'm sorry." Faden's voice was low and his eyes began to well up.

"Your brother's an animal." Tommie's own voice was unsteady.

"I'm sorry," Faden said again.

"It wasn't your fault," Eva said gently. She looked at Benedict. "You know, this is where fighting gets you," she said. "Do you see what you started?"

He didn't know this girl enough to care what she thought about him, but her words still stung. His lip was already swelling into a giant ball.

When Eva looked at his wound, she shook her head. "This is bad. Martha and David are not going to like this at all. Not at all."

Benedict sat slouched on his bed with his packed bag next to him. He was holding a bag of frozen peas against his lip when Sebastian appeared in the doorway to announce that Martha and David wanted to see him. *This must be the quickest transfer in the history of foster families.* He picked up his bag and made his way slowly down to the kitchen.

David stood in front of the sink while Martha paced the floor. Nana Credence was there also, sitting at the table, her lips curved down in sadness. Benedict looked around the room for Miss Davis, but she was not there yet. He usually felt nothing during these moments, but for some reason, in Martha and David's home, he felt a weight in his chest. He was short of breath, and felt a large lump in his throat that was impossible to swallow. He sat down and Martha glanced at his bag. Her eyes welled up and she looked at her husband.

4

D AVID BEGAN by clearing his throat.
"Benedict, we were saddened when we heard about the fight today," he said. "I realize that Martha and I never discussed with you that fighting will *not* be tolerated, and we're aware that you've had many issues with fighting, but that was in the past."

"Benny, I'm sorry that boy said those awful things." Martha interrupted her husband. "A happy person would never be so cruel."

"Needless to say . . ." David resumed his lecture. "You need to find better ways to resolve your issues, do you hear me?"

Benedict waited for him to continue, but he didn't, so he slowly nodded his head.

"Good." David nodded. "Now, I hate to do this to you, because you just arrived here, but I will have to ask you to return to your room for the rest of the day and think about how you could have dealt better with that situation."

Benedict looked at David, Martha, and Nana Credence in turn, then back at David, who nodded toward the stairs. "Go on now."

He stood up hesitantly and picked up his bag.

"Benedict?" Martha called as he walked away. "Is that your laundry or were you planning on leaving us?"

He looked down at his bag, but didn't say anything.

"Leave the bag," she said. "I'll take care of it."

He dropped the bag and headed up the stairs to the bedroom, where he lay on his bed facing the window. It was his first day here at Sunshine Ranch and he had already caused trouble— but he was still there.

"Hey," a voice whispered behind him. He looked back to see Sebastian. "They weren't too hard on you, were they?" He shook his head and the older boy smiled and gave him a thumbs up. Benedict turned back to the window and smiled.

***

AS EVA ENTERED the bedroom she shared with Tommie, she noticed her roommate staring at her reflection in the dresser mirror. But she hurried to her closet and pretended to be busy looking for something when she noticed Eva's presence.

Eva had seen the troubled expression, but said nothing as she picked up her favorite music box, wound it a few times, and set it down. It released a soft melody and she smiled. As she began brushing her curly blond hair, her gaze wandered to the dresser.

"Tommie!" She spoke her foster sister's name through clenched teeth. She had left the dresser in perfect order that morning, but now her side had been invaded by Tommie's items.

It was the perfect representation of their room as a whole. On Eva's side, the bed was dressed in white, with powder-pink embroidered edging. Her bedside table was covered with a white cotton doily. On it were her lamp, a music box holding her rosary, and a Bible. Each item was in its respective place and, even on dreary days, the sun always seemed to shine brighter on her side of the room.

In contrast, Tommie's bed was in disarray, her dark blue duvet cover still pulled back from when she'd woken that morning, and clothes from days before were draped over the footboard of her bed. Comics, books, and shoes scattered the floor.

"Tommie, why do you leave a trail of destruction wherever you go?" Eva placed one hand on her hip and gestured around the room with the other.

Tommie looked around, and Eva could tell that she was still upset about what happened in town. But she didn't know what to say about that, so she tried to change the mood. "I mean, didn't we agree on our own sides of the dresser? So why's your black mascara, black eyeliner, and . . . what is . . . ?"

She picked up a small item, but after a closer look, she gasped and dropped it. "Ewwww! Tommie, what have I said about this?"

Tommie went over and picked up her spare nose ring, spinning it between her fingers and staring at it gloomily.

Eva sighed and sat on her bed, looking at Tommie. "You know that Roy Simms is a fool," she said casually.

"I don't care about Roy Simms," Tommie said quietly, her eyes not leaving the spinning nose stud.

"Then why do you look so miserable?"

That question seemed to wake Tommie from her trance. She looked fiercely at Eva for a second before she gave an exaggerated sigh and threw her arms up in frustration. Then, muttering to herself, she stomped over to her bed and began pulling the blanket up in a lame effort at making it. Finally, she grabbed her clothes, threw them into the closet, and shut the doors as far as the shoes obstructing them would allow.

"You know, Eva, you've become more annoying since you turned fifteen." She narrowed her eyes, looked at her foster sister, and added, "You're not perfect."

Eva felt those words more than any other. She decided not to say any more. Instead, she got up and walked calmly out of the room.

Tommie sat on her bed. She was sorry for hurting Eva's feelings, especially since her foster sister was just trying to be kind, but she couldn't tell her the truth. That would have been even worse.

***

AS THE DAYS and weeks passed at Sunshine Ranch, Benedict allowed himself to relax, if only just a little. Melanie's transition was much quicker, and he couldn't help but feel a tad envious that she seemed at home in the arms of Martha, and Nana Credence, and David, and even "Bones," as he liked to call Mr. Jones.

Even after Martha had washed his clothes that first time, he had still rolled up each article and packed them into his bag. Every night, he took out his pajamas and put his dirty clothes in the hamper. In the morning, he took out the clothes for the day and rolled up his pajamas and any clean clothes before packing them. Then one day, almost two months after arriving at Sunshine Ranch, without reason or provocation, in the midst of rolling his pajamas, he stopped abruptly and folded them instead. Then he placed them in the top drawer of his bureau and looked at them for a moment before closing the drawer.

However, any speck of serenity in his mind was short-lived. About a month later, his fears resurfaced at the arrival of twin babies, Peach and Tobiah. Then, just three weeks later, on an uncharacteristically stormy day in early June, they were reorganizing rooms because a new boy was to arrive—a boy of ten, just like him. A boy who could most certainly be chosen over him, should the need arise.

"Tell me again why I have to switch rooms?" He stomped through the hallway, balancing a badly stacked pile of books in his arms. Martha stood against a wall, making way for him. Melanie skipped past them, carrying a pillow.

Martha sighed and threw him her warning look. "Please don't make me answer that question for at *least* the fifth time, Benny."

"Benny, you're getting a bigger room." Sebastian spoke in an equally exasperated tone as he came out of his room carrying a little girl over his shoulder. "You just have to share it."

He handed the giggling child to Martha. "Guess who was in my closet, again?"

"Oh, Francine." The two-year-old girl grinned as Martha brushed black hair from her face.

"Oh, and it's leaking in my room again."

"It's raining?" Martha muttered the question and the toddler giggled her response. Isabella pushed by Benedict carrying Tobiah awkwardly around the waist.

"There's a storm a-brewing, didn't you hear?"

Martha winced at these words and Sebastian's smile disappeared. He made a face of regret. Benedict snapped his gaze to Isabella.

They all hoped Isabella hadn't heard, but sure enough, the girl had stopped mid-step and turned back to them, eyes wide with fear.

"Storm?"

Tobiah stuck his fingers in her open mouth.

Sebastian mouthed, "Sorry," to Martha and escaped downstairs, muttering, "I'll just go find a saucepan now."

Benedict groaned, fully aware that his protests had been set aside for bigger concerns. He sighed loudly for effect and marched off.

"Why get another kid if we don't have the space?"

When he reached his new room, he let the books drop to the floor with a thunderous bang.

David raised his eyebrows while he screwed a wheel onto the bottom of Benedict's bed.

"We just got Peachie and Tobiah." Benedict raised his hands. "Nine kids aren't enough?"

David smiled. "Not for Martha."

"You don't get a say?"

"Well." David rested his arm on his knee. "Can I be honest with you?"

Benedict nodded eagerly.

"I kinda love all you guys, too," he whispered.

Benedict's eyes narrowed and he shook his head. "Well, you're no help."

David just smiled and then pointed to the books.

***

"MRS. CREDENCE, I was just checking in to see if Mr. Credence was still picking up little . . . uh . . . Mike . . . Micah . . . yes . . . little Micah. The little Irish boy. What with the impending storm—although some are saying that it'll pass your neck of the woods."

It was Miss Davis on the phone. Martha had been expecting the call. It came every time a child was placed with them, usually on the day of arrival.

She took a deep breath. "Oh, yes, he's already on the road. We're very excited." She stirred a pot of boiling potatoes.

"Great, great. And how are the little African-American babies doing?"

She rolled her eyes and her mother-in-law, who stood at a counter chopping an onion, smiled sympathetically. Ma was just as familiar with these conversations.

"Peach and Tobiah are also doing great."

"Excellent, excellent . . . and the children we placed with you a few months back . . . the Italian boy and the French girl?"

"Benedict and Melanie . . . their names are Benedict and Melanie and they're fine, Miss Davis . . . as is my Chinese girl, Francine, my American-Indian girl, Tommie, and my all-American children, Sebastian, Eva, and Isabella."

Ma placed her forefinger on her lips and frowned at her sarcasm.

Martha bit her lip and closed her eyes. Lord, forgive me and bless me with patience.

"Yes, you have yourself a little United Nations going on there, it seems." Miss Davis laughed softly at her joke before saying goodbye.

Martha groaned as she put the phone down and leaned against the counter, her lips turned down in playful regret.

Ma just shook her head before draining the large pot of boiling potatoes, diverting her face from the rising steam.

"Sorry, I just get so frustrated with that woman." She casually picked up the mail and glanced through it with a creased brow and a slow shake of the head.

"Has David heard about the John Miller team yet?" Ma asked. "It's that time, isn't it?"

"No," Martha replied absently. "And, yes. It couldn't come at a better time." She sighed loudly before tossing the bills back on the counter. "Pray with me, Ma, that the team comes in soon. We need it more than ever this year, what with all the repairs and especially with that roof. That's going to take a pretty good chunk."

In response to her words, the wind howled outside and

she looked out at a storm-infested afternoon. It hadn't missed them, it seemed, but rather it had crept up on them and was at that moment dumping its wrath upon them. At one moment, the trees swayed, and at another they shook brutally. What scared her most was the way they bent as far as physically possible, straining against the strength of a ruthless wind. All the while, the rain poured down, changing direction according to the gusts, each drop slamming hard against the walls of the house.

Martha grabbed the phone and tried David's cell phone, but it didn't connect. She tried a couple more times, to no avail. She looked at Ma, who stared out the window with a pained expression.

"Martha, Martha," a voice called.

"Little Bella," she whispered. The little girl was so afraid of storms that she would hyperventilate if no one held her throughout her ordeal.

Isabella ran into the kitchen and into her arms.

"It's okay, little one." But she wasn't sure she was telling the truth. Suddenly, she felt so vulnerable.

The kitchen door flung open and they all jumped, as a drenched Mr. Jones burst in. Martha grabbed the kitchen towel so he could wipe his face. Isabella followed her every move like a devoted puppy.

"It's pretty wild out there," Mr. Jones reported between heavy breaths. "I secured the barn though. Should be okay."

Ma put the kettle on and Martha looked at her watch. David was probably on his way home, but he'd still be at least an hour away. The lights suddenly flickered, and Isabella screamed. Martha directed the child to her mother-in-law and went to the pantry, where she retrieved some emergency lanterns and their radio. The lights flickered again and the three adults exchanged nervous glances.

"I think we should gather the kids in the great room," Martha said. "If the lights go out, it could be chaos."

The storm proceeded incessantly, and Martha's nerves were worn thin. She wanted to pace the room, to cry out loud and call out to David. But she couldn't do any of those things, because she would scare the children and they were anxious enough for her.

Tommie and Benedict tried to play chess, and Sebastian tried to read to Peachie, who kept turning the pages prematurely; and Isabella couldn't get close enough to her Nana, who also had Tobiah on her lap. Melanie sat with Mr. Jones and Eva, while Francine held onto Martha. Music played in the background to cover the noise of the storm.

"Oh, Lord." Martha tried to keep her voice from shaking as she prayed aloud. "Protect David and Micah. Please don't let anything happen to them. Return them both safely to their family. I beg of you, God." She continued to pray to herself.

Eva also prayed, and Nana Credence, and some of the others, because that was all they could do. It was all in God's hands now. And then the lights went out.

5

FOR THE SHORT moment that they were in darkness, and the music was silenced, they were consumed by the brunt of the storm. Wailing filled the air, along with the consistent rattling of rain thrashing against the sides of the house, and a rhythmic banging. Some of the children screamed, which made the babies cry, and the adults rushed to quiet them down while Sebastian and Mr. Jones turned on the lanterns. Their florescent glow filled the room, and Eva turned on the radio. It was all too much for Martha to bear. She needed David there, and if he didn't come home soon, she was going to die from the anxiety of the unknown.

At that moment Tommie, who had been staring out of the window, yelled, "They're here, they're here." They all rushed to watch as two bright lights flickered through the moving tree branches, blurred by streaks of rain, and then descended the hill slowly.

Martha thought she'd never heard more beautiful words. She giggled like a little girl and let out the breath that she'd been holding in. Then, handing a sleepy Francine to Eva, she grabbed a lantern and rushed to the front door. She didn't have to look back to know that they had all followed her.

It was only a few moments before the door burst open and David came in with a young boy wrapped from head to toe in a long jacket and blanket.

Martha didn't even give her husband a chance to remove his wet coat, and she didn't care that she was soaked by his embrace. Then the others joined in and David was swamped, until he was forced to gently pry them off and remind them all that he had Micah with him.

"Children, this is Micah," he announced, as he removed the jacket and blanket that covered the boy. "Please make him welcome."

Martha reached out to him and held the child's sullen face with her hands.

"Micah."

She whispered his name and looked into the shivering boy's watery gaze and her heart ached for him. She knew his story, and she could read it in his eyes. He'd lost his parents a few years back and then, more recently, his grandfather, whom he equally loved and adored.

"Welcome." She tucked a lock of brown hair gently behind his ear and then stood aside to allow the others to say hello. But he didn't respond. He just stood there, his green eyes welling with tears.

Ma rushed to get a warm blanket, and Martha led Micah to the great room. The others shuffled behind and, when they had settled down, David recounted their adventure. They no longer heard the storm outside or cared that the lights were out. David was home. As he talked, Micah sat next to him, wrapped in a dry blanket, silent and without expression.

After the winds had died down and night had settled in, the children felt safe enough to go to bed. The younger ones, including Isabella, had already fallen asleep. David and Sebastian carried them to bed. Mr. Jones would remain at the house for the night, so Eva brought him a pillow and some blankets.

David signaled quickly to Benedict, who stood up reluctantly. "Benny, come with us and we can show Micah your room."

***

THE BOYS TRUDGED up the stairs and down the hall to the bedroom in silence. David dropped Micah's bag on his bed and watched as the boy looked absently out of the window. Benedict looked out over the boy's shoulder. The darkness hid the extent of their land, and the effect of the storm taking its toll on it. A dull banging broke through the sound of the wind, calmer now, and David peered out into the night, a frown wedged on his brow. He instinctively checked to be sure that the window was locked before turning to Micah. Benedict sighed, placed the lantern on the dresser, and sat on his own bed.

"Don't be afraid to ask for anything." David spoke in a low voice. "Things are pretty laid back during the summer. I'm sure the kids will fill you in."

Micah didn't respond. David walked over to the boy, put his hand on his shoulder, and turned him around to face him.

"I can't imagine how hard this is for you," he said softly. "I promise I won't pretend I can, but please remember this, Micah: I will always be here for you. We *all* will."

Benedict knew that David's words were honest. He also knew that Micah was not ready to believe them.

Once David had left, Benedict watched Micah unpack his clothes and place them in his dresser.

"Would you like some help?" he asked half-heartedly.

The boy shook his head. He was careful not to unfold the items that he removed from his suitcase. He picked them up one by one and placed them into the drawers, not once acknowledging Benedict, who was watching his every move.

From among his clothes, Micah pulled out an old camera and two framed pictures. He looked at the photos for a few moments before placing them on the table next to his bed.

Benedict couldn't see the images clearly from where he sat. When Micah had finished, he closed his case, shoved it under the bed, and left the room, carrying his pajamas and toothbrush. Benedict chose this opportunity to get a closer look at the pictures. One image was of a much younger Micah with a couple who Benedict assumed were his parents. The mother sat on a grassy spot with her husband behind her and their little Micah perched on her lap. The other picture showed an old man in wading boots and an older Micah holding up a small fish.

Before Benedict had a chance to return to his bed, Micah was back, but he simply glanced from Benedict to his pictures.

When Benedict lay back on his bed, he said nothing while Micah stood by his own bed, as if waiting for something to happen. Then, to Benedict's annoyance, he dropped to his knees, clutched his hands together and rested his forehead on them. *Great. Another one.* But then he thought about it more and decided that he too would probably pray if it meant that he got to stay at the Ranch. *But who's listening? A God who chose to give this kid loving parents and not me? What if this kid gets to stay and I don't? What if they pick me to leave, because they realize there are too many kids?* The questions swirled around Benedict's head, making him giddy. Micah climbed into bed.

Benedict thought of what life would've been like if he had had parents who loved him. He searched his mind trying to remember them. But only remnants of memories revealed themselves to him, like pieces of an old puzzle that offered only fragments of the full picture. He thought about how murky his entire journey had been, from one foster home to another, until it brought him to where he lay now. Benedict fell asleep with that thought in his mind and the sound of calmer winds whistling outside. And Micah sobbing into his pillow.

***

THE *RAP, RAP, RAP* of hammering resonated throughout Sunshine Ranch, and paused when David sat up to wipe his brow on his shoulder. He rolled his neck in circles to ease the pain, before glancing at the farm from his panoramic view.

The sun was shining overhead and the sky was blue. It would have been hard to believe that a storm had engulfed them the night before, if not for the trail of destruction left behind. The corral had blown over, with sections twisted and mangled; both the barn and the house suffered extensive roof damage; pieces of fencing had dislodged from the main field; and they lost five large trees, not to mention a mass of tree limbs, branches, and shrubbery littering the grounds.

David looked down at where Mr. Jones was trying to replant a pear tree that he and Martha had put in the day they'd moved into Sunshine Ranch. No one was sure if it would ever bloom again, but they had to try. Luckily, though, the old oak had come out of the storm unscathed. As had the family, his mother had reminded them all. David took a drink from his water bottle and returned to work. Below him, inside the barn, the children were performing their Sunday morning chores.

**

"TOMMIE, DID YOU get Red and Captain yet?" Faden's face appeared over the door of the stall she was mucking out.

She stood up straight and leaned against her shavings fork. She was on the last stall. There were only five to clean although the full capacity of the barn was twelve.

"No, but check with Sabe, he might have."

Faden lifted his cowboy hat and wiped his forehead with the back of his hand before disappearing.

There had been no discussion regarding the incident outside Milly's Café. It was as if it had never occurred. No one could feel bad about it if they remained silent.

Tommie sighed softly before she scooped the last of the soiled wood shavings into the wheel barrow and steered it out to the walkway.

Benedict passed, leading a white mare out to pasture, Micah by his side.

"So most likely it'll be a bigger team than last year," Benedict was saying, as if he were a veteran at the farm and an expert in its business proceedings. "They always are."

Micah quickened his pace, trying to keep up. Benedict didn't look at him as he talked, but marched along with his chin lifted high and his posture straight, as David had instructed them all.

"You know, the team comes all the way from California. That's 'cause David's so good at breaking horses. He's going to teach me one day, y'know."

Tommie smiled and shook her head as she watched the boys head out of the barn.

Faden appeared again, carrying a bag of shavings, which he emptied onto the floor of the stall. Tommie fluffed the shavings with her fork and spread it out evenly.

Just then, Melanie and Francine shuffled by, pulling a bucket of water and spilling most of it along the way.

"You guys need a hand?" Tommie asked, grinning.

"We've got it," Melanie panted.

Sebastian appeared from the stall next door.

"Thanks." He grabbed the bucket from the kids, looked inside, and frowned. "At this rate we'll get the horses fed and watered by next year."

The others laughed.

"They insisted on helping," Tommie said, adding, "You guys want to help me feed Captain Jack?"

"Yeah," the little ones said in unison and skipped after her.

"Breakfast!" Eva could be heard calling from the house.

The hammering stopped.

"Let's get going, guys," David called out as he descended the ladder. "We don't want to be late for church."

***

SAINT PATRICK'S CHURCH stood tall in the small New England town. As the church bells rang, the Credence children marched down the aisle in their usual scattered formation. Martha and David carried the twins, Isabella held Francine's hand, and Sebastian carried a sleeping Melanie.

Tommie and Faden exchanged a wave. Benedict and Roy scowled at each other.

Finally settled, they listened to Miss Virginia Madden playing the old piano while the procession made its way up the aisle. Benedict watched Mr. Jones close the doors, adjust his old worn out jacket, and take his place in a nearby chair. Once seated, he "rested" his eyes, but his ears were wide open. At least that's what he'd told Benedict, when he asked the old man why he slept during Mass.

Fr. Thaddeus waited politely for Miss Madden to finish the hymn. Eva sang along, closing her eyes and lifting her chin in reverence, while Tommie shook her head, clearly embarrassed. When Miss Madden was finished, she paused slightly, her fingers still on the keys and her head bowed for a moment before she turned in her seat and looked at Fr. Thaddeus. He returned her gaze over his glasses and nodded, as if to ask if she was ready. She smiled at him triumphantly and nodded back, permitting him to begin.

The ceremony proceeded as always. Benedict began his usual check-off procedure in his mind: *blessing, first reading, blah, blah, blah, Miss Madden sings, of course all I can hear is Eva, second reading, blah, blah, the Alleluia, the Gospel, the homily, blah, blah, blah, blah, Our Father and peace be with you, blah, blah, the Eucharist while Miss Madden and Eva sing again, the final prayer and blessing and then Miss Madden sings while everyone slowly proceeds to the exit, greeting each other along the way, while we have to drag Eva out, la de dah done.*

He was restless for it all to be done. His mind wandered back to that morning when he had given Martha a hard time about coming to church.

"Why we gotta go to church *every* Sunday?"

"Little Ben, why do I have to *explain* it to you *every* Sunday?" She turned him around and led him back to his room.

"Church won't make me believe in God." A scowl creased his forehead.

"No, I don't expect that it will, but going to church on Sunday is what this family does and you are a part of this family." She went into his closet to find his clothes.

"Why?"

"Please don't whine, Little Ben . . . because it gives us an opportunity to acknowledge, praise, and thank God."

"Well, when I get to decide it, I'm not going to church on Sunday. It's *boring*."

"Well, I'm sorry you feel that way, but when you are old enough to decide it, that will be your prerogative."

"My what?"

"Your choice." She looked at his scrunched up face and kissed him on the forehead. "I love you, Benedict, whatever you decide, but I do hope that one day you realize God's love and how amazing it is."

And so here they were again. Benedict tried to stifle a yawn. Fr. Thaddeus was in the middle of his homily. This and the preparation of the bread and wine were the longest parts for Benedict to endure, but the latter also meant the service was almost done.

"We were all born under different circumstances, this is true," Fr. Thaddeus was saying. "We're all different, whether in ability or even opportunity. Our struggles are different. Some of us are financially more secure than others. Some of us have had more education. Some of us have more help than others. But none of these conditions determine our future."

Benedict looked around; at Eva who was completely engaged; Sebastian who wore a frown; and Micah who looked at peace. When Benedict looked at Eva again, she was glaring back at him. He shrugged and tried to pay attention.

"Regardless of our situation, we *all* have to make the right choices to better our lives. But it takes passion and a lot of work. And it takes faith. With God's help, there's no limit to what's possible. We just need to accept God into our hearts, and have faith in Him, and call out to Him."

At the end of the service, the children waited and

watched while Nana Credence and Martha lit candles at the back of the church. After a few minutes of prayer, Nana left her daughter-in-law's side and Martha remained, head bowed, hands clutched, while the children waited. After the other parishioners had greeted the family and left the church, Fr. Thaddeus came back in. He and David talked briefly, waiting for Martha, who was taking much longer than usual. Melanie and Francine chased each other around Sebastian's legs.

"I think Peachie needs a change," Eva whispered.

Benedict heaved a sigh and David and Nana Credence exchanged a serious look. Finally, David went to his wife, put his arm around her waist, and whispered into her ear, before leading her back to her family.

***

"GIVE IT TO ME. Come on, give it to me." Tommie watched as Benedict followed Micah with his hand extended. She knew what he wanted—the green and yellow striped photo album his new foster brother had tucked under his arm. Martha had given it to Micah after she learned that he enjoyed taking pictures. It had become apparent to Tommie in the days following Micah's arrival that Benedict didn't like him much.

The children, including Faden, sat watching the commotion from the porch. Micah walked fast around the yard in a zig-zag pattern, now clutching the book to his chest, and looking back at his pursuer with an almost amused expression on his face.

"I just want to look at it for a second," Benedict said, through gritted teeth.

He quickened his pace, but Micah managed to dodge his every reach, until Benedict finally stopped, placed his hands on his hips and yelled, "This isn't just your house! Besides,

I've been here longer than you, so you need to listen to me."

Micah stopped too, panting a little harder than Benedict, and shrugged his indifference. For the next moment, they faced off.

"Hey, Benny," Sebastian called, "Cut that out." He was feeding Tobiah a bottle.

"What?" Benedict turned to him, his hands raised in question. "I'm just filling in Micah over here on the rules." He squinted from the sun.

"Those are not the rules, Benedict." Eva didn't look up from painting her toenails a pale pink. "Now stop being a bully."

Benedict turned to glare at Micah, who was staring back at him without any expression. He shifted from one foot to another and then let out a big sigh, and with his finger pointed toward Micah's face, saying, "Just stick to the rules," before he walked off toward the back of the house.

Micah stood alone, seemingly lost at what to do next.

"There's no such rule," Sebastian called to him. "Benny's just being . . . Benny."

"Yeah, he's annoying, but Martha says he grows on you," Isabella told him and shrugged, clearly not convinced that this theory was actually true.

"Not sure exactly when that's supposed to happen," Tommie chimed in. She looked at Faden, who was now watching Eva painting her toenails while he absently plucked at the strings of his guitar.

"Eva, who are you trying to impress?" Tommie asked.

Eva rolled her eyes. "You, Tommie." She spoke without looking up and then giggled at her joke.

"Well, it just doesn't match your Catholic girl persona." Tommie chuckled softly. She looked up discreetly at Faden, who seemed oblivious of their conversation.

"What's that supposed to mean? Catholic girls can't wear nail polish?"

"Yeah, you're a Catholic, aren't you?" Sebastian interjected casually.

"I'm not over the top about it, though."

"What does that even *mean*?" Eva now glanced up at Tommie, her eyes narrowed in accusation. "You're either a Catholic or you're not."

"Oh, man," Sebastian said, "something stinks in Suburbia." He lifted Tobiah into the air, his face twisting in disgust. He looked over at Isabella who was reading. "Mama Bella," he cooed.

Isabella looked up to see him holding the squirming Tobiah out in front of him and jumped up enthusiastically, to grab the baby from him.

Eva looked at him with her mouth open, and when Sebastian saw her face, he shrugged and asked with a mischievous grin, "What? She doesn't mind."

Isabella was inside the house in seconds.

"Poor Bella. You guys need to stop using her." Eva's face was angry.

Sebastian and Tommie exchanged mischievous looks.

"Who's that?" They all looked to where Micah was pointing up the hill. At the top of the driveway, a man stood gazing down at the house. No one recognized him, and no one liked the way he seemed to be surveying the property.

Sebastian stood up and walked off the porch, his eyes never leaving the man. "*Hey!*" he yelled up at the stranger.

The man turned to them, but he didn't shout or signal back. Instead, he hurried to his car and drove away.

6

LIKE MELANIE, MICAH had no problems adjusting to the Credence home and family members, much to Benedict's aggravation. He got on well with the others, and even though he'd lost the most precious people in his life, he was genuinely content.

He was thinking about just this as he leaned against the open kitchen doorway and looked out at the sunny day. Benedict, Eva, Tommie, and Isabella were with him in the kitchen, packing for a fishing trip.

"You know what this place needs?" he asked. He scratched his head through his worn out fishing hat and stared out at the old crooked oak tree.

"Another boy to tell us what we need?" Tommie muttered, without looking up from organizing her fishing tackle.

"No, but on that note, a boy to replace Benedict would be second on my list."

"Ha ha." Benedict pushed his jaw out. He threw a worm at Micah's head. "You're a scream."

"No, this place needs a treehouse." Micah picked the worm off his hat and put it in his bait box. Then he pulled his camera from his pants pocket and took a picture of the tree.

"Oh, yay! How great is that idea?" Isabella clapped her hands in delight and looked around for supporters, but nobody bit, so she went back to spreading peanut butter onto slices of oat bread.

He took a picture of her, and then one of Eva trying to stuff a pillow into her backpack, before leaving the room for more home comforts.

"Sounds like a lot of work to me, and it's way too hot for a lot of work." Tommie slung her pack over her shoulder and headed out the kitchen door to put it with the rest of their equipment. Benedict threw another worm at Micah's head, and this time Micah gave him a look of warning.

"Come on, it would be so great, and I know the perfect tree." He looked back at the old crooked oak, with its huge trunk and large branches reaching out, as if begging for a treehouse to embrace. It *was* the perfect tree, but still no one seemed to budge.

Although Isabella showed some promise, he knew that he would need more than her help if Sunshine Ranch was to see a treehouse any time this century.

Tommie walked back in through the door, and as she passed, a worm slapped against her cheek. She, Benedict, and Micah all gasped at the same time.

"Cut it *out*, Benny." She picked the worm from her shoulder and threw it back at him.

"Benedict." Martha walked into the kitchen with Peachie in her arms. She placed the baby in her highchair, just as Nana Credence walked in with Tobiah and placed him next to his sister. Martha went on to say, "I love you, but if I hear one more complaint about you today, you will be grounded."

Micah took a picture of Benedict pouting and then another one of him glaring at him.

The previous grievance had been by Isabella, accusing Benedict of prodding her in the arm after he lost at a game of checkers. Before that, Tommie had mentioned that her comics had been rifled through, although Eva asked her how she could tell. Now Benedict just stood dangling a worm from the tips of his fingers.

Mr. Jones entered the kitchen from the living room and helped himself to a glass of water. The AC had broken that morning, for the third time in as many weeks. As usual, Mr. Jones did what he could, but when Martha looked at him now, he glanced back and said, "Probably the last time that trick will work."

"Don't worry, guys." Martha turned back to feeding Peachie. "Once the California team arrives, we'll get a new AC. That one must be over ten years old."

"When will they call?" Tommie asked.

"It should be any day now. You know Mr. Miller, he always calls last minute and expects the whole team ready before the summer's up."

At that moment, Eva rushed in, out of breath. "Martha? Martha, someone's been in our room. My music box is broken."

She held her prized possession out to Martha and turned the handle to prove it wasn't working. Martha took the box and turned the handle, also.

"I know it was working last night, it was working just fine." Eva's voice was a high pitch and her eyes were flooded.

"I can vouch for that." Tommie raised her hand and rolled her eyes.

Eva tried to steady her voice. "You know I love my music box."

Martha looked at the children around the room and then her gaze stopped on Benedict. "Well?"

Before Benedict could say anything, Micah threw his hand up. "I did it!"

Benedict turned to him, his mouth open.

"I'm so sorry," he said, shifting his eyes from Eva to Martha. "I saw the box and I just wanted to hear what song it played." *Forgive me, Lord.*

Eva sighed and told him that it was okay, but her eyes were sad. It was easy to see that she was heartbroken.

Mr. Jones took the box from Martha and turned the defective key. When Eva asked if he could fix it, he nodded and said he probably could make it work again.

Micah could still feel Benedict staring at him, but he kept his eyes on Martha. He braced himself, feeling a lecture coming on, but the tense moment collapsed when David marched in through the kitchen door.

"We ready to fish?" David's grin disappeared after he saw the sullen faces. But when he asked if everything was okay, Martha sighed and told him that everything was fine. Before she could explain what had just occurred, the phone rang, and she rushed out of the room.

***

"OKAY, CREDENCE FAMILY." David pierced his bait. "You heard Martha. We're not allowed home until we've caught enough fish for dinner."

The group was on the lake, split into two rowboats bobbing in the water. David was with Sebastian, Tommie, and Isabella. In the other boat, Mr. Jones, Eva, and Benedict began casting their lines, and Micah was taking pictures.

Eva smiled and sucked in the smell of summer and sunscreen. "Okay, team, let's show them how it's done."

"You talking about us?" David called over to her, mimicking a tough-guy voice. He cast his line.

"I sure am," she said with equal conviction, and readjusted her fishing hat.

"You talking about us?" David asked again.

"Did I stutter?"

"Ooh, them's fightin' words." He raised his eyebrows and looked at the others in his boat. "We gotta beat them, team. You hear me? She's acting a little too big for her britches."

"Just making it interesting," Eva yelled back with pseudo-confidence. Then, to Mr. Jones, Benedict, and Micah, she added, "We can do this, team. Wha'dya say?"

"Hey, I'm all for it," Micah said with a wide smirk. He tucked his camera away and cast his line.

Benedict and Mr. Jones sat back and waited for that first bite.

"Losers clean the whole catch," Tommie yelled to them.

"I *like* that." David nodded with a grin.

The teams settled in their boats, quiet on the outside and basking under the same sunny blue sky, but each mulling over their own thoughts.

Eva adjusted her pillow and prayed that her team would win the fishing contest (she hated the feeling of fish scales), but then she felt bad about the motive behind the prayer.

Tommie prayed for the same thing, but figured God wouldn't mind.

Sebastian was still wondering who the man at the top of the driveway was. He'd mentioned the incident to David, but he didn't seem that surprised.

Micah gave in to the impulse of reliving a memory of him and his grandfather fishing the previous summer.

Benedict kept recalling the moment Micah admitted to breaking Eva's music box.

David was trying to calculate the financial burdens incurred by the June storm, on top of the already growing repairs, and then he prayed Mr. Miller would call soon.

Mr. Jones felt the weight of it all.

***

Three hours later, David's team sat scaling fish in the yard just outside the kitchen door, while the other lounged inside, cooling off in the air-conditioned kitchen. David asked whose bright idea it was, and he, Sebastian, and Isabella looked at Tommie, who pretended not to hear the question.

"We couldn't just *lose* at the fish count; you had to have a *consequence*." Sebastian flicked a fish scale at Tommie, who in turn flicked one back at him and reminded them that they had all been in agreement at the time.

"Well, that was *before* we lost." David smiled. "Here, why don't you take these in to Martha to start washing?" He handed a tray of scaled and gutted fish to Tommie, who grabbed it gratefully. Isabella offered to help and followed Tommie into the house, carrying a large fish with both hands.

As soon as the girls were out of ear shot, Sebastian said, "Note to self: Tommie's bright ideas aren't so bright."

David chuckled as he sliced his fish. "Hey, we only lost by two. That's not bad."

"Thanks to you."

He smiled and watched the boy continue to debone his fish with an expert hand. "Well, I appreciate that, but it works both ways. I have great students."

They worked quietly for a moment before he added in a lower voice, "Actually, I have great kids."

Sebastian didn't respond. His jaw tightened and his smile seemed strained. But before David could ask him if he was alright, Tommie and Isabella returned, Martha with them, carrying a tray of drinks.

"David, are we done now?" Tommie waved a fly away from around her head. "I'm hot, AC's dead, and I want to swim a bit before supper."

"AC's dead?" He looked up at Martha, who nodded and handed him a drink. "Well, you have one more." He pointed to the bucket where a lonely fish waited. Tommie threw her head back in exasperated fashion.

Isabella reached into the bucket. "I can do it for you."

"You will?" Tommie beamed, but then catching sight of David's concerned look, she added quickly, "Oh, she doesn't mind. Besides, she debones a fish so much better than I do." Isabella was already busy at work.

"Then, I guess you're off the hook." He shrugged and Tommie ran off into the house. "Mr. Miller call yet?" He already knew the answer to that before Martha shook her head. He returned to his work and she touched his head gently.

***

THAT EVENING, the smell of grilled fish and bug spray saturated the night air. The Credence family sat around the oversized picnic table under the old crooked oak. Tiny lights filled the branches and hung overhead, extending all the way to the top of the kitchen window. Soft music played in the background. The only other sounds that mixed in the evening air were those of clinking cutlery and murmurs of appreciation.

Micah took his last bite and leaned back in his chair. He looked up at the old crooked oak and once again envisioned it cradling a treehouse.

"Don't even think about it," Benedict said.

"What?" Martha glanced around the table confused.

"He's thinking about the treehouse again." Benedict pointed at Micah with his fork, rolled his eyes, and groaned.

Micah shrugged. "What's wrong with that? It's a good idea. You're just mad because it wasn't yours."

"*No,* I just don't see the fun in spending the whole summer building a treehouse that none of us will really get to use."

"I'll use it." Isabella raised her hand.

"And me." Tommie shrugged. "It could be fun."

"Yeah, it'll be a *blast.*" Benedict rolled his eyes again. He looked up to the sky and shook his head. "Besides, that's *not* even what I meant."

"You're such a grouch." Eva shook her head.

"Fine, you do what you need to do." He leaned in and glared at Eva. "I'm not wasting my time. I doubt I'll be here long enough to care." With that, he left his seat and went into the house.

At that moment the phone rang and David jumped from his chair, still chewing his food. "I'll get it," he said before anyone else had a chance to.

***

"BENEDICT?" MARTHA followed the boy inside, but he headed to the bathroom where he locked her out.

"Little Ben," she called through the door. "You know you really shouldn't miss out on having fun just because you're afraid the fun won't last."

She leaned her forehead against the cool, wooden door and waited, but he didn't respond. "Honey, just know that I pray you're mine forever."

She stood by the door a few minutes longer, trying to coax him out. But it was to no avail, so she headed back outside. On the way, she noticed David sitting quietly in the living room. She'd heard the phone ring as well, and now she was anxious to find out if it was Mr. Miller.

"Was it about the team?" Martha asked her husband. The room was dim, but she could still see his sullen expression. Her heart began to beat fast. She moved slowly toward him and knelt in front of him.

"What is it, David?"

7

DAVID HAD BEEN DREADING this moment, but he forced himself to look his wife in the eye. "There won't be any team. Miller said he's going to use somebody closer to home." He swallowed the bitter taste these words produced. No horses to break, no income. Sure, from Miller's point of view, it made perfect sense—he probably got a great price from the young upstart he'd chosen to hire, and he saved the price of transporting and boarding the horses, as well. But didn't he realize he was taking food out of the Credence family's mouths? Eight horses—that would have paid enough to keep them going for months. "What a find," Mr. Miller had said. "I'm sure you understand." David had said that he did, while at the same time, he had felt his insides collapsing.

***

TOMMIE PERCHED on the corral fencing, watching Faden work.

"It's all about how to control without using strength." Faden led Captain Jack, a chestnut gelding, recently brought to Sunshine Ranch for breaking. He wore his cowboy hat slanted low over his eyes, and Tommie could just see his mouth move as he spoke. "Horses are strong animals, so there's no point in trying to control one by pushing it around. You're going to lose. Course Captain's a gelding now, so he's calmer than he was as a stallion. He's just got a few bad habits that need breaking."

She admired the confident way he projected himself, and she wondered why he wasn't as assertive when it came to Roy.

"Is this the 'man's not stronger than a horse' lecture?" She tilted her head to one side and narrowed her eyes in suspicion. "You sound like David."

She was immediately sorry for her words when she saw Faden's lips tighten.

"Well, David's the expert at calming lively horses." He backed off his assuredness. "'Course I'm going to sound like him, if he's the one who taught me all this stuff."

She felt bad for putting him on the defensive. "I was kidding."

He just shrugged and continued on without a word. Captain Jack walked proudly around the corral. He had a long handsome neck that blended nicely into his withers, and his head bobbed along with each step, while his tail whipped at every fly that found the nerve to move in too close. His body was as slick as ribbon candy and his black mane was brushed to silky perfection. He was a beauty; his conformation almost perfect, but for the bow-knees on his back legs. He couldn't be a show horse with that flaw, but he would do well as a police horse, once his temperament was under control.

"So, how do you get a horse to change its wild ways, anyway?" Tommie laughed at her question, because it sounded so silly.

"You gain its trust and then its respect," Faden said, adding in a low voice, "David told me."

Tommie bit her lip. She didn't have the nerve to now suggest to him that it sounded a little too horse-whispery for her. Besides, she thought, there had to be something to the process, since most of David's clients trekked across the country for his services.

As if reading her mind, Faden said, "You know, I won't be working here much this season, just a few hours here and there." Tommie hoped he hadn't seen her jaw drop, but he wasn't even looking at her. "Shame about the California team."

"David won't need you?" Her voice was a higher than normal pitch, even though she had wanted to sound casual. She recalled David saying there would be some sacrifices, but she never guessed one of them would be Faden.

"Just here and there, at least for now."

At that moment, Captain Jack stopped walking. Faden clicked his tongue but the horse stood still.

"What happened?" Tommie asked. "Is he looking at me?" Her eyes narrowed and she pulled her head back.

"No, I don't think so."

"Uh, yeah . . . I think he is," she said nervously. It wasn't that she was *afraid* of horses. She rode often, in fact. She was just a little uneasy around the wild ones.

"He's not looking at you." Faden clicked again and this time yanked the reins gently to get Captain's attention.

"He's totally looking at me." Tommie was about to climb off the fencing when the horse trotted toward her. She leaned back a little, but that little was just too much and she lost her balance, falling to the ground with a big thud.

Faden leaped over the fence and was standing over her in seconds. "You okay?"

She just groaned and looked up at him. His head was

haloed by the sun behind it and she couldn't see his expression until he knelt down next to her.

"You banged your head. You okay?" He looked concerned.

"I'm fine." She was embarrassed and tried to get up quickly, but it made her dizzy, so she lay back down.

"Hey, take it easy." Faden glanced at Captain to make sure the horse was okay and then looked back down at her.

"I'm fine!"

He helped her to a seated position. "That was a pretty bad fall. You want me to go get Martha?"

She smiled now, because he'd pushed his hat up and she could see his full face. She'd never noticed his summer freckles, and he looked younger without the hat tipped low. His eyes were wide as they stared directly into hers, and she had to divert her own gaze, praying her face wasn't as red as it felt.

She searched the back of her head for a lump, but there wasn't one, and the dizziness had subsided.

"No, I'm really fine." She'd fallen on grass so she wasn't too worried.

Faden waited a few more seconds, nervously turning a silver band he wore on his left hand.

Tommie suddenly felt self-conscious with him so close to her. *Why's he staring at me like that?* She didn't like it.

Unexpectedly, he asked, "Did that hurt?"

"No, I'm *fine*, I said!"

"No, I meant *that?*" He pointed to her nose piercing, and then pulled his hand back quickly.

She covered her nose with her hand and frowned over it.

"I'm sorry. I didn't mean to embarrass you."

"I'm not embarrassed. Why would I do it if it was embarrassing?"

"I didn't mean that, I meant—don't—I just don't want

you to think it's weird."

"It's weird?" Her eyes widened over the hand that still cupped her nose.

"No, not that, I just didn't mean to be nosy." He laughed awkwardly.

Tommie was completely horrified. Suddenly, Faden's face was his brother's that day in town when he said those awful things.

Faden hit his forehead with his palm and shook his head. "I'm an idiot," he muttered to himself, and then he looked into her eyes and said sincerely, "I'm really sorry," and she could see that he really was.

"*What's going on?*"

They both jumped to their feet, not just because the voice had surprised them, but because it belonged to Roy.

"Tommie had a fall," Faden answered and signaled over to her. "She banged her head."

She wished he hadn't said anything about it, but she knew also that he was in an awkward position, so he'd better have a good explanation.

Roy just glared at Tommie and then at his brother and commanded, "Let's go."

Almost a week had gone by since the nose ring incident with Faden, and Tommie was still bothered by it. She leaned in toward the mirror above the dresser and stared at herself, her eyes focused on the ring as she backed off and turned to her side, assuming a serious face without any expression. *It's not that bad.* She crinkled her nose. Then she reached up and removed the ring. She made more faces, looking at her nose from various angles, and sighed.

She gazed down and saw Eva's items neatly placed on her side of the dresser: perfume, pale lipsticks that Martha just started allowing her to use, pink and white brush, and tiny earrings.

Tommie remembered Martha's words when she first arrived at Sunshine Ranch. "I have to tell you that I don't approve of the nose ring or the makeup, but I'm not going to change who you are. We'll take you no matter what. You take your time. I just hope that one day I can meet the real you." She had smiled when she said it.

Tommie still didn't understand what she'd meant when she said that. She looked at herself again, the nose ring, the black around her eyes, the dyed hair. This was who she was, or at least it was who she had to become in order to survive. This was her protection every time she ran away from her mother's home and walked the streets at night. No one approached her when she wore boys' clothes and gothic make up. She couldn't be a girl out there alone, and she certainly couldn't stay at home.

She had run away from her home so many times she'd lost count. The first time was the scariest. It was like a whole other breed of people came out at night. It wasn't long before she was found, however, and at that time, she was relieved. The second time she ran, she dyed her hair with red streaks and dressed like a boy. And the third time, she pierced her own nose and dressed like a Goth. She had never gone back to her old look. Now she stared at herself and a feeling of anxiety overcame her. *Lord, you love me no matter what I look like, right?*

She looked down at the dresser again and picked up Eva's pale lipstick. She leaned in and tried it on, just as Eva walked into the room.

"That's a pretty color." Eva smiled.

Tommie jumped away from the mirror, dropped the lipstick, and wiped her lips with the back of her hand, all in one swift motion.

Eva's jaw tightened and she lifted her chin. "Lunch is ready," she said stiffly, and then she turned on her heel and left the room.

A sound from outside caught Tommie's attention and she looked out of the window to see David and Faden finishing up their work. She watched a little longer.

***

"WHAT'S MICAH DOING?" Tommie asked as she pegged a sock to the line.

She, Sebastian, Eva, and Benedict were hanging out the laundry for Nana Credence because, much to Martha's dismay, the dryer had broken down. Isabella was nearby, directing Melanie and Francine in a dance move, but the little ones were more interested in escaping and running through the wet sheets. At Tommie's words, they all froze mid-action.

They watched as Micah emerged from behind the red barn, awkwardly dragging a long piece of wood toward the old oak tree. At one point he turned, readjusting his hands so he was pulling the wood and walking backwards, but that method proved too difficult, and so he readjusted again. He didn't stop until he reached the old crooked oak, where he dropped his end of the plank and returned to the barn, his head hung low.

Micah's desire to have a treehouse had quickly become an obsession. It seemed to him that on any given day, the others had some excuse or other not to get up and help. One day was too hot for Eva, another, too cold for Benedict. Either Sebastian was too busy or Tommie was too tired. Day after day, the excuses piled on and eventually Micah took matters into his own hands.

"He's not seriously going to try and build that on his

own is he?" Eva looked nervously from Sebastian to Tommie.

"It'll take him years," Tommie said.

"Anyone going to help him?" Isabella was still panting from running after the girls.

"Why don't you?" Benedict asked.

She pointed to herself, her eyes wide and mouth open in shock at the suggestion. "I'm the littlest one."

Micah reappeared from behind the barn with another plank and headed back toward the tree. Sebastian looked at Eva and shrugged, as if to ask if they should help.

"It's so hot today," Eva whined.

He sighed. He wasn't in the mood either. In fact, he had hoped that after hanging the clothes, they'd all go for a swim.

Suddenly, they heard Martha's voice from the kitchen, calling Micah. She came running out the door toward the young boy, who had now stopped halfway between the tree and the barn. Micah waited for her to reach him, his hands behind his back, clutching one end of the plank. The children couldn't hear what was being said, but from Martha's flailing arms, it was obvious that she wasn't very happy with him. Micah, in response, shrugged every now and then and shook his head in intervals, and finally stood staring at his feet before dropping the plank behind him and heading inside.

After watching him walk away, Martha headed over to the other children.

"I think this idea about a treehouse is great," she said, "but I won't have Micah working on it alone." She gave them all a meaningful glance, then turned to go back into the kitchen.

Once the laundry was hung, Sebastian, Eva, Tommie,

Benedict, and Isabella found Micah sitting alone on the top step of the front porch, staring sullenly at the ground. Although the others felt bad for him, no one offered to help continue his project that day. It was just too hot.

"Well, I hope you're happy?" Benedict said as they all settled around him. "You just got us in trouble."

"No, I'm not happy." Micah didn't look up.

A silver Cadillac made its way down the long dirt driveway. Mr. Jones, who was watering the still dormant pear tree near-by, stopped and watched along with them.

"Who's that?" Tommie asked.

"There's only one man in town who drives a flashy set of wheels like that," Eva said.

Sebastian got up and headed into the house to inform Martha of the visit, while the others continued to watch Mr. Green, the bank manager, exit the car and climb the porch steps. He ran a palm over his slick, dark hair and smiled at them.

"Good day."

"Good day," they responded in a ragged chorus.

He and Mr. Jones nodded their greeting just as Martha appeared at the front door with Sebastian behind her.

"Hello, Mr. Green, what a pleasant surprise." But it didn't look like a pleasant surprise to the children. With some hesitation, she showed him into the house.

Sebastian sat back down. He didn't like the heavy feeling that had set in his chest. He glanced at the others who were now quiet, each likely wondering why Mr. Green was inside their home right now.

Except Isabella. She was looking out into the sky. "Look at that." She pointed to a collection of clouds that hovered in the deep blue sky over a distant mountain. From an opening somewhere within the clouds, rays of sun burst through and spread out below in a majestic fashion.

The children gazed for a moment in silent awe at the vision. Mr. Jones looked up also.

"Wow," Tommie whispered.

"That's amazing," Sebastian said.

"That's heaven." Micah spoke matter-of-factly.

"What?" Benedict looked at him, scrunching his nose in response.

"Heaven—and God's peeking through." Micah knew it to be true.

"You're nuts." Benedict shook his head and snorted.

Micah shrugged, untouched by the insult. "That's what my grandpa used to say."

"Well, your grandpa's nuts," Benedict said, without thinking. This time Micah frowned and pursed his lips.

Sebastian pushed Benedict. "Cut it out, Benny."

"My Grandpa's dead," Micah said sincerely.

"You're a real knucklehead," Tommie said through gritted teeth.

"Knucklehead," Isabella repeated, pulling Francine's finger from her nose.

"It's okay," Micah said. "He's there when I need him."

Benedict was sorry that he'd called Micah's grandpa nuts, and he wanted to say so, but it didn't feel right to. He decided to let it go, and so he joined the others, who had resolved to remain in silence, watching the summer day continue on in its usual unhurried fashion.

A squirrel ran past the porch and up a nearby maple tree. It paused halfway up its trunk only a few seconds before disappearing into its leaves. The sudden squeal of the screen door indicated that Mr. Green was leaving, and reminded those children who had forgotten, that he was there.

Both David and Mr. Green walked out and stood side by

side, silently gazing toward the mountains. David turned to stare briefly at the children, before dropping his gaze with an air of defeat. Then he turned on his heel and headed back inside. Mr. Green spent a few more moments scanning the property before getting in his car. The children watched as he drove away, crunching up the drive.

Later that evening, after supper, they all gathered in the great room.

Sebastian sat on the couch. "There's a show tonight?"

The others followed suit, finding comfortable spots.

Benedict dumped himself into a bean bag. "A show? Oh, great."

"Give it a rest, Benny," Tommie warned. "Bella works hard on these."

In fact, Isabella was all director, choreographer, costume designer, and dancer in these shows, which occurred at least once a month now.

Once the audience had settled, Isabella entered the room wearing Eva's old white chiffon dress that reached the floor, and she took her place in front of them. Francine and Melanie followed, and all three waited for Sebastian to turn on the music. Tonight the song was Amy Grant's "El Shaddai," and Isabella began to lip synch the words and dance around in ballet style, her dress floating with every turn. As she reached her arms out in reverence, the little ones moved their arms in more of a hula-dance fashion that made everyone exchange glances and stifle laughter. At one point, Melanie fell while twirling, causing the audience to laugh louder, so she and Francine continued to fall "accidentally" for the effect. Isabella didn't notice, but danced on until the music ended, and then she and the little ones bowed.

Benedict rolled his eyes and glanced over at the others. In that moment, he saw David reach out for Martha's hand and squeeze it—not an unusual gesture on his part, but Martha's sad eyes when she looked at him sent a shiver through Benedict. It was a feeling he hadn't felt in a long time.

"Great, can we go to bed now?" He stood up and left.

***

ISABELLA WATCHED FROM the window as Micah pounded nails into a plank. Suddenly, he collapsed, and Faden, who had agreed to help him for the day, rushed over to him.

At first, Isabella thought Micah had just fallen backward over something, but when he didn't get up, she ran through the house and out the kitchen door yelling, "*Micah hurt himself.*"

Martha dropped what she was doing and ran after her.

8

BOTH DAVID AND MARTHA spent the rest of the day at the hospital, leaving the house quiet and full of unanswered questions. Finally, that evening, the door opened and David walked in, his eyes bloodshot and his hair rumpled. Questions erupted from the children as they crowded his path toward a seat.

"Quiet," he said, in an attempt to settle them. "Okay, okay, let me in and I'll try and answer your questions."

Nana Credence quieted the children, allowing her son to settle into his chair. When he was seated, his coat still on, and the children had settled quietly around him, he cleared his throat and told them that they needed to be brave

Those words instilled the opposite emotion. Eva begged him not to say anything bad, and he shushed her gently, then explained that Micah had a weak heart. His voice cracked as he spoke and he took a deep breath to compose himself.

Eva, sitting close to him, reached out to touch his hand. He smiled at her and then at the rest of the children, but his eyes were dull. When Isabella asked him when Micah was coming home, he twisted a button on his coat and then stood up.

"We're not sure yet." His usual strong demeanor had returned.

Isabella burst into tears.

"Come here, Mama Bella."

She rushed into his open arms.

"We all need to be strong for each other." He shifted his glance from one child to another and kissed Isabella on the top of her head. "I love you guys, you know that, right?"

They nodded.

"I love you all so much and I need you to be strong." He kissed Isabella again. "I must get back there. I came to get clothes. Please be good for Nana. It may be a few days."

Sebastian told him that they'd be fine and David held his gaze and nodded. Sebastian seemingly understood the message in his eyes—that he would be the man of the house until David returned and, in this crisis, he wouldn't be invisible. Benedict was silent the whole time.

The next morning, the children were roused by the sound of hammering. Isabella ran to the window, desperate to see Micah, but was surprised to find Benedict working on the treehouse.

Slowly the children emerged from the house, rubbing their eyes and yawning. Benedict didn't notice them at first, and then he looked up, eyes narrowed and blazing.

"All he wants is a treehouse," he said angrily. "A treehouse." The admonishment was intended more for himself than for the others. He shook his head.

After a moment, Sebastian walked over and touched his shoulder. They exchanged a somber look.

"Don't cry," Sebastian whispered, and then he picked up Micah's blueprints and surveyed the tree.

All the children, including Faden, helped Benedict and

Sebastian finish Micah's treehouse. It took three full days. Mr. Jones showed the children the correct way to saw the wood and to use the tools. He even painted the finished treehouse with a protective coating. Nana took charge of feeding them, comforting them, and nursing wounds.

***

Martha and David were away for four days before they brought Micah home. The boy seemed even thinner than usual. David directed him right through the house and into the backyard where the others were gathered beside the large picnic table. Preparations for a barbeque lunch were underway.

At first, Micah didn't notice the construction because he was too busy hugging the others. But then, as they watched him with shared amusement, he looked up and saw it, right there in front of him.

The wooden structure sat snugly in the arms of the old crooked oak. There were two screened windows on opposite walls dressed with bright orange shutters, and the main door on a third side led out onto a generously-sized deck, half the size of the treehouse itself. Mr. Jones had carved balusters for a railing on either side of the deck, and at the front hung a rope ladder, secured to the ground at the bottom. Isabella had insisted they add a tire swing below for "something else to do."

Mica gazed at it in amazement. "I can't believe you guys finished it."

They were all inside the treehouse now, settled in a circle and staring cheerfully at each other. Micah's smile was weak. The color was still drained from his cheeks and he had needed help climbing the ladder, but it was evident that this was the happiest he'd ever been for as long as they had known him.

He sat on a purple cushion that Eva had found in the attic and gazed at the photos and drawings that Isabella had posted on the walls around them. Mr. Jones had also made a small book shelf for their comic books and had given them an old lantern that Sebastian hung in one corner.

Isabella was animated as she explained to Micah that finishing the treehouse was Benedict's idea. Micah frowned at Benedict, who just shrugged and mumbled a comment about being sick of all the whining, and that he still thought it was a dumb idea. Micah laughed softly and told Benedict that he'd so missed his cheerful disposition.

It was Sebastian who suggested they christen the treehouse with a camp-out that very night. Since it was Micah's first camp-out with them, Isabella took it upon herself to inform him that they usually set up tents in the field past the barn, and then they'd stay up all night playing truth or dare and eating s'mores.

Benedict scoffed as he listened. He told Micah that, in fact, in the couple of times he'd camped with them during the spring, Isabella didn't last long. David usually had to walk her back to the house before it got too dark because she was scared of the night critter sounds.

Eva warned him to stop being unkind, and then Tommie confided to Isabella that she, too, was scared of animal sounds in the night, especially bats.

"I get freaked out by that squeaking sound." Tommie shivered at the thought. "Man, it creeps me out."

At that moment, Martha called up to them that lunch was ready, and so they all descended the ladder.

"Get down, Bella." Benedict nudged Isabella toward the ladder. "Go on, you first."

"No, you first." Isabella nudged him back.

"You're right there, you go on," Benedict said through gritted teeth.

"I want to go last."

"Well, I want to go last, too, so you need to go." He poked her in the shoulder.

"Why do I need to go?" She raised her voice and rubbed her wound.

"Hey, what are you two doing?" Sebastian called up.

"Look at that." Tommie pointed to them. "Benny and Bella sitting in a tree, K.I.S.S.I.N.G . . ."

"Cut it out!" Isabella yelled as she descended quickly down the ladder.

"Hey, that ain't funny, you guys." Benedict followed, his face distorted with an expression of disgust. The others laughed.

"It got you out the tree though, didn't it?" Sebastian said.

That evening, two tents stood rigid beside the old crooked oak, and the campers sat mesmerized by the crackling flames of an open fire—all except Micah, who gazed up at the treehouse, now covered in the lights that once illuminated just the tree. The boys would sleep in the tents and the girls in the treehouse, it was decided.

Faden joined them, and Tommie was glad to see him and his guitar. David had already walked Isabella in, to Benedict's obvious amusement.

Tommie broke into the peaceful moment. "Okay, are we playing this dumb game or not?"

Eva gave her a perplexed stare. "Well, if it's such a dumb game, why do you want to play it?"

"It's better than sitting in silence."

"Actually, it's not." Eva slapped a mosquito on her leg.

"Actually it is," she mumbled in the hopes of getting the last word. The others ignored them. Tommie looked up at Faden, who sat leaning back in a beach chair, strumming softly in the night air, and watching the flames flicker and spit.

"You know, anytime you feel like going to bed would be *fine* with me." Eva tossed her hair. She was desperately trying to remain calm.

"What and miss out on your *stimulating* conversation?"

"Why don't you both just give it a rest?" Sebastian interrupted. His face was rigid in the glow of the flames. He paused a moment, as if daring one of them to challenge him, but neither did."

"You kids alright?" David's yell came from the kitchen door periodically.

"Yes!" They all yelled back.

Faden cleared his throat. "Okay, so —"

"Pick dare, pick dare, pick dare," Benedict whispered in the background.

"Truth," he decided.

Benedict groaned and threw a twig in the flames.

"I have one." Eva raised her hand into the air. "How come you're so sweet and your brother—"

"Is such a *cretin*," Benedict sneered.

"No." Eva threw him a glare. "That's not what I was going to say," she said to Benedict, and then she turned to Faden with an apologetic look and repeated, "That's not what I was going to say."

"That's what you were thinking," he muttered, picking up a stick and snapping off a piece.

"Benny!" they all shouted.

"Benny, why do you have to be mean all the time?" Eva asked.

"I'm not being mean. I'm just saying it as it is. Sometimes the truth hurts." He threw another piece of stick into the flames.

"You think God would approve of your behavior?" Eva asked.

"Who cares?"

Eva looked at him, her eyes wide in horror. "How can you say that?"

He just shrugged and continued to throw pieces of stick into the fire. He didn't have to look at Eva's face to know that her cheeks were flushed a bright scarlet. He wanted to laugh as he imagined a vein throbbing on the side of her head, just like in a movie he'd watched recently.

"You could go to hell if you keep talking like that."

"You're nuts, Eva." He tried to sound unaffected, but secretly he wondered if she was right.

"Eva," Sebastian interrupted.

***

Eva's heart beat faster than normal in her chest. "I'm not nuts," she said softly.

"Eva . . . Eva?" Sebastian kept saying her name until she turned to look at him, her eyes filling with tears. "Stop," he told her.

She did stop, and she was glad Sebastian had told her to, because she would have burst into tears the next time she opened her quivering lips.

"Eva . . . it's great to love God, but you can't make others love Him," Sebastian said kindly. Eva nodded, biting her lip and thinking for a moment. "You've heard the expression, 'you can bring a horse to water, but you can't make it drink?' This is the same thing."

She took a deep breath. "I'm just helping us to be good people." She spoke in a low voice.

"Yeah . . . well, it's not your job," Tommie said abruptly.

"It's so annoying, she, like, prays every second she gets." Tommie laughed and looked around at the others, as if trying to rally up support.

"You're not perfect," Benedict interjected.

"I know that," she muttered and lowered her head.

"Okay, who's next?"

"Fine, it's my turn," Sebastian said. "Dare . . . what do you have for me, Benedict." Eva knew that Sebastian was willing to do anything to lighten the mood.

"Okay, okay." Benedict bounced up and down with excitement. "I *dare* you to run around in circles yelling, 'I'm a fruitcake' at the top of your lungs."

"What?" Sebastian frowned, while the others laughed.

"Go on, you have to do it, Sabe," Benedict insisted.

"Fine . . . how many times?" He lifted himself from his camp chair.

"Three times around."

Sebastian started running around them. "*I'm a fruitcake!*" he shouted. "*I'm a fruitcake, I'm a fruitcake . . .*"

The others laughed hysterically. It was ridiculous, but equally hilarious.

"You kids alright?" David called from the house.

"*I'm a fruitcake,*" Sebastian yelled back.

"As long as you're alright!" David responded, to which they all burst into more uproarious laughter.

Finally out of breath, Sebastian collapsed in his chair. "You're in for it." He pointed at Benedict.

"Eva's turn," Micah said.

Eva looked at him. "Dare."

"I have one," Faden said playfully. She waited. "I dare you to sing."

"What?" Eva's heart began beating fast again.

"Sing." Faden dragged his fingers softly over the strings of his guitar for effect. "I've heard you belt it out in church. I'd like to hear you sing."

"I can't sing." Eva looked to the ground.

"Doesn't matter, it's the dare." Faden was teasing her now, unaware that the thought was terrifying her.

"You can sing," Tommie said, without much enthusiasm.

"Yeah, you should hear her in church; she's like the loudest one."

"Be quiet, Benedict," Sebastian said.

"Eva's mom used to sing," Tommie blurted out. Sebastian kicked her leg. "What?"

She raised her hands with a 'what's the big idea' glare at the boy.

"Sing, Eva, sing," Benedict began to chant.

"I don't even want to play anymore," Eva said quietly.

"Neither do I." Sebastian stood up. "I say it's time for s'mores."

***

Benedict complained that he hated s'mores and instead had a hankering for an ice-cream sandwich. Tommie reminded him that he already had one for dessert, but he muttered that it was a celebration, so Martha wouldn't mind.

Still, as he neared the house, he lightened his footsteps and turned the handle of the door carefully. The kitchen light was off, so if he reached into the freezer, he could be in and out in no time.

Inside the dark kitchen, Benedict noticed a flickering light coming from the living room and heard hushed conversation. He stopped in his tracks. The voices continued softly and he crept carefully toward the living room, lowering himself to the floor as he got closer.

Martha and David sat facing each other across the coffee table. Candles flickered around them. Martha sat on the edge of her armchair, her hands clutching a cup as she waited for David to finish writing something in a book.

"If I do it any other way, I'd be making it up, Martha."

David leaned back on the couch. "The repairs from the storm cleared our savings. We needed Miller's team to . . ." Benedict couldn't make out the mumbled remainder of the sentence.

"We have to make it work." Martha's voice was urgent.

"How, Martha? How do we do that? We're so far behind and it's so late in the season."

"I know. I'm sorry." She took a deep breath. "It's just that . . . it feels like everything's falling apart and we can't lose this house."

9

BENEDICT'S HEART JUMPED at the words, "Lose this house."

"Oh, David. How could this be happening?"

David and Martha sat quietly for a moment in the flickering candlelight. Benedict couldn't see their faces clearly, but the quiver in Martha's voice made his stomach flutter.

"Okay," David whispered. "I have to find a lucrative client, that's all. We still have a little time. We can't lose faith. God's helped us through harder times, right? He'll help us through this." But even Benedict wasn't convinced by David's words, because they didn't match his voice.

"I know." Martha set her cup down and rubbed her hands together. "I'm worried because it's not just you and me anymore, David. And what about Micah?"

What about Micah? Benedict wondered, as he remained crouched in the darkness. He wanted to cry out. He wanted to run to them and beg them to keep the house. *Why would they lose it?* He wondered if he should tell the others.

"What was that?" Martha looked up, startled.

Benedict held his breath, afraid he'd been discovered,

but then he heard another sound.

"Bella," Martha whispered and ran from the room.

Benedict backed further into the shadows until Martha was passed him. He was familiar with the sound of Isabella sobbing, and he'd seen Martha many a night, sitting next to the child's bed, stroking her hair and singing, "Bella . . . Bella . . . Mama Bella . . ." while he secretly watched. He didn't know Isabella's story, and he was glad for it, because crying every night had to mean that genuine pain was trapped in Isabella's heart.

Once Isabella had settled back down and Martha had returned to David downstairs, Benedict crept up to his bedroom. He couldn't face the others, and he was sure they wouldn't miss him, anyway. As he lay in his bed, the words *lose this house* and *what about Micah* swam around in his head. He wanted immediate answers to his questions, but that would mean admitting that he'd been listening in on David and Martha's conversation.

When morning finally came, he descended the stairs, expecting to find everyone assembled and waiting for a family meeting. But Martha, David, and Nana Credence were the only ones drinking coffee at the table. When Martha saw him enter the kitchen, she smiled and reached out to him in her usual manner, and he went to her and kissed her cheek. The older children began to enter from outside. David looked at his watch and raised his eyebrows, as if surprised at the time. He mumbled something about a lot of work to do, and after greeting each child, he left the room, and Martha began to take breakfast orders. The morning resumed as usual.

***

A few days later, when the Credence family had just finished dinner and was settled in the great room, Sebastian was putting away the last of the dishes when David entered the kitchen, waving an envelope and sporting a big smile.

"What do you say to you, me, and the Sox next weekend?"

Sebastian looked confused.

"I have an old school buddy in the city who gets season tickets," David explained. "I gave him a call last week and he offered up two tickets for us. Come on, just you and me. It'll be a good opportunity to catch up on some, uh . . . father and son type stuff."

At first, Sebastian just shifted from one foot to the other. He opened his mouth to speak, but then closed it just as quickly. It sounded great to him. He wanted to go, but when David had added the "father and son" comment, Sebastian felt a warm sensation rush through him. . Finally, he said, "I don't know," and turned away.

David was now the one left with his mouth open. Sebastian didn't want to have to explain that the invitation was bittersweet, because he didn't know if his reasoning even made sense.

"What's going on, Sabe?"

David's voice was soft, but Sebastian detected the crisp, stern tone. He knew he'd have to explain sooner or later, but it have to be later, because just then Tommie entered the kitchen and informed them that Mr. Green had come for a visit. David sighed, then turned and walked out.

***

TOMMIE WATCHED in the hallway while David smiled politely and shook Mr. Green's hand.

"We can go into the study," David said. "Can I get you a drink?"

"That's not necessary," Mr. Green looked around. "This shouldn't take long."

Tommie tried to find reasons to stay in the vicinity of the study door. She couldn't hear what was going on inside the room, except for some mumbled voices, but she wanted to see the outcome of the visit. She paced the hall for what seemed like an hour, recognizing raised and hushed voices. Eventually, the door opened and she rushed to find an excuse for still being right there. The men stopped and watched her spin on her heel and pretend to walk casually toward the kitchen.

"Milk," she said with a nervous smile. "Peachie wants some milk." She walked off, but not before she noticed that Mr. Green was smiling and David was not. Tommie was suddenly afraid.

***

DAVID SLAMMED the receiver onto the phone and rubbed his face with his hands. He couldn't remember when he had ever spent so much time calling horse farms and riding schools across the country, or any other place that required the use of a horse breaker. The last call, like so many of the others, had seemed promising for jobs in the future, but what he needed was work *now* to cover the loss of Mr. Miller's California team. He sat back in his chair and recalled the meeting he and Martha had had with his mother.

She had revealed to them that she'd saved some money over the years and, although it wasn't enough to buy the house, it could keep them afloat, at least until David found enough work. It would at least buy them some time, she had reasoned. She understood that Christmas wasn't a good time to find his kind of work. Even now David felt an ache in his chest. How could he take his mother's money? But she'd threatened to leave unless they were willing to allow her to "do her part," so they had reluctantly agreed.

He kept wondering how long they could maintain the appearance that everything was okay. At the sound of Isabella laughing in the great room, he smiled sadly. *Lord,* he prayed, *I feel that You're challenging my patience and faith, and I'm afraid. It's getting harder and harder, Lord.* He heard his own words echo in his mind and shook his head, suddenly ashamed.

"I can do all things," he said to himself.

The phone rang and he started. Miss Davis' greeting caused his heart to sink deeper. He knew her questions because she'd just asked them earlier that week and the week before, but still he had no definite answer for her. She was concerned and needed to know if she had to transfer the children. He assured her that that wouldn't be necessary.

"We'll find a way," he had said. "So you needn't worry about the children." He slammed the phone again. His eyes stung. He closed them tight and whispered, "I can do all things."

"David?"

He opened his eyes to see Tommie standing at the doorway, staring at him with wide eyes and a trembling bottom lip.

"Worry about the children?"

"Oh, for goodness sake, that's nothing for you to worry about." He stood up and adjusted his papers aimlessly. "You know the state always calls to check up on you guys. It's fine, really."

He walked over to her and kissed her on the head, not once looking into her eyes. "It means they care," he concluded and walked past her.

"David?" Her soft voice was a whisper and her face

wore a petrified expression.

"Yes?"

"Would you and Martha lie to us?"

"No." He said it without turning around so he didn't have to look into her eyes.

***

Tommie rolled onto her left side for what seemed like the hundredth time and stared through the darkness of the room past Eva's bed, and into the night. As the breeze reached in and touched her face with the tips of its essence, she yearned for more. She wanted to lose herself in the sensation. She wanted to fly out into the night and glide peacefully like Peter Pan. But the state of her mind was far from the tranquility that she wished for. She was anxious and afraid and she was wide awake. She had prayed until she could find no other way of begging God for a miracle. He knew what she wanted, she decided. He knew what they needed, and so it was all on Him now.

David's face was still ingrained in her mind. His awkwardness and lack of eye contact made her afraid. And when she had asked her question, her heart had beat fast, and when she tried to swallow, her throat had gone dry because she knew it wasn't a polite or even respectful to imply, but she'd asked it anyway.

"Would you and Martha lie to us?"

His answer had been no—but the way he said it communicated the opposite.

She turned onto her back with a sigh and looked up at the ceiling, and then back onto her side, until one moment became too much for her and she slipped out of bed and put on her slippers. *It's not enough.*

"Eva." She whispered into the darkness, shaking her foster sister gently. Eva groaned, pushing a defiant hand in her direction and turned away. Tommie shook her harder.

"What?" she hissed.

Tommie knew that sleeping was Eva's favorite pastime and all efforts to remain composed were forgotten if she was disturbed. Tommie knew this, but she didn't care.

"Get up." She shoved her harder.

Moments later they crept through the house, quietly waking the others.

***

"IF WE LOSE this house, we'll be split up, you know."

Benedict scowled at Tommie's words. She had summoned him, Sebastian, Eva, Micah, and Isabella to a secret conference in the treehouse. Sebastian had lit the lantern, but dimmed it as much as he could so that it wouldn't be obvious to Martha and David that they were there.

"I thought that if we had 'faith,'" Benedict gestured quotation marks for effect, "Everything would work out?" He raised his eyebrows as if to catch Tommie in a contradiction.

"That's true, Benedict, but in the mean time we can't just sit around waiting for God to fix things. We have to do our part."

"If we don't make an effort to fix things, why should we expect God to help?" Isabella asked with a shrug.

Eva leaned against the wall with her arms folded and her eyes blinking slowly.

Benedict rolled his eyes and turned his attention to a swarm of moths and night beetles collecting on the window screen next to him. Although he pretended not to be scared about losing the house, he really was. He also wondered if he should tell the others about overhearing David and Martha the other night, but they'd probably yell at him for snooping.

"I'm not ready to leave this place." Sebastian said.

"We know." Benedict chuckled and looked around for support, but no one complied.

"Are *you*?" Sebastian asked with accusing eyes. Benedict didn't respond.

Tommie resumed her leadership role. "We need to save Sunshine Ranch, so we need to make money."

"How?" Sebastian asked.

"Well, that's why we're here." She looked at them each in turn. "To put our heads together. Wake up, Eva."

Sebastian leaned over and nudged a sleeping Eva, who jolted at his touch. Her eyes opened, but they were bloodshot, and her blank expression indicated that she was clearly not awake.

Sebastian snapped his fingers in an obvious attempt to ignite motivation and inspiration amongst the fading group. "Okay, so we need ideas."

Benedict looked around, but Isabella was now drawing a picture of the family members, Micah was stifling a yawn, and Eva had rolled into a fetal position. He turned his own attention back to watching the screen.

Sebastian clapped his hands to get their attention. "Come on, you guys! How important is Sunshine Ranch to you?"

"Well, obviously, since we're here in the dead of night, it's pretty important," Benedict said.

"Yeah, that's apparent." Sebastian signaled to Eva and Isabella, but then he sighed and shook his head. "Maybe we're making a big deal out of nothing."

"Yeah, maybe they're just a little strapped for cash." Tommie's mood lightened a bit.

"Yeah, or maybe they're about to lose the house," Benedict said.

Silence ensued.

"I heard them the night of the campout," he admitted. "The storm took their savings, and they lost the Miller team, and now they might lose the house." He wondered if he should mention the *what about Micah* comment, but decided against it.

They looked at each other in silence.

"Why didn't you tell us?" Tommie asked angrily.

"He just did," Micah said quickly.

Sebastian shook his head adamantly. "We can't let that happen."

"Well, then we have to make enough to cover the savings!" Micah said.

"How about a yard sale?" Tommie threw out, smiling.

"That's dumb," Benedict responded almost immediately, and then reached out and flicked at the screen, sending the insects bouncing out into the darkness. Micah laughed and Benedict realized that he'd been watching. He chuckled and watched a collection of more insects mindlessly gather, ignorant of their fate.

"We don't have enough stuff to sell to make much." Sebastian looked at her, his expression twisted, as if sorry for having to agree with Benedict's thoughtless retort.

"I could do a show and sell tickets," Isabella said casually, her head tilted to one side as she colored her picture.

"Ooh." Tommie's eyes widened. "That's it. We should have a show. Kinda like Bella's shows, but bigger, like a variety show. We can take donations, have a raffle, we could get Faden's band to play, horse riding . . . it would be so fun. And if everyone comes, we could make some good money."

Micah's eyes widened. "It'd be great. And we could each do something. Sabe, you can show off some of your lassoing tricks that David taught you . . . make a big show of it. Benedict, you think you're a comedian, so you can tell some jokes. Eva could sing. Tommie you can . . . what can you do?"

"She could be a mime," Sebastian responded.

Tommie frowned at Sebastian, who shrugged his apology.

"Eva won't sing, by the way," Tommie said.

"Why?" Micah asked, but Tommie just shook her head and left it at that.

"I want to dance. I want to dance!" Isabella clapped her hands excitedly.

"I don't know." Sebastian frowned. "A variety show?"

"Yes," Tommie said. "We'll have a variety show, and we'll call it the Credence Variety Show."

"Oh, *that's* original."

"Be *quiet*, Benedict."

10

EVA WAS HORRIFIED when Tommie broke the news to her about the Credence Variety Show. She thought it was a ridiculous idea but, more than that, she was afraid when Benedict told her they'd voted for her to sing. She refused outright. She didn't want anything to do with it. But the others said that she had to do her part in saving Sunshine Ranch, so she agreed to help with costumes.

"But that's it!" She threw her palm up in the air as if to fend off further objection.

The next concerning matter was getting permission from Martha and David.

***

When Sebastian and Tommie had shared their plan, Martha and her husband exchanged a sad glance.

"We want to help," Isabella insisted.

"Let us think about it, and we'll let you know."

They did think about it, and argued about it, too. David insisted they should let the children follow through on their plan, but Martha continued to resist. Finally, he took her hand and gazed steadily into her eyes.

"We have to let them do it."

She sighed. She was tired. She looked at her children, who were playing a game of tag football, and then at her husband, waiting for her response.

"David, it'd be a drop in the ocean. I just don't want their hopes to be raised and then dashed away."

"Are you losing faith?"

She smiled at him and squeezed his hand gently. "No."

They watched the children chasing Benedict and laughed softly.

"They need to do this for some reason," David said. "And we shouldn't deny them. We're still here together."

Sebastian dived out with his arm extended and grabbed Benedict by the leg, planting the boy face-down onto the ground. "Ouch."

Martha stood up. "Is he okay?"

She sat back down when Benedict got to his feet and dusted himself down before turning on Sebastian. The others yelled and cheered after them.

"This is our life," she said with determination, and David nodded with a smile.

Looking at her husband, she tried to see the child she'd met all those long years ago. And although he was hidden now behind the strong chin, the graying hair, and the impending wrinkles around the eyes, she saw him most definitely in his smile. That smile. She remembered the first day she saw it when he put sand in her lunch in kindergarten. She chuckled to herself as she recalled his reasoning.

"What?" David asked with a furrowed brow.

"*Sand*wich." She shook her head and looked at him with a smirk.

First he was confused, but then he understood and laughed at her playfully, as if the incident had just taken place.

***

"THAT'S THE LAST ONE," Sebastian said to Tommie as they exited Milly's Café. They looked at the poster she'd just taped to the inside of the window, advertising the Credence Variety Show on orange craft paper. *The Credence Variety Show: Ride, Dance, and Be Entertained,* it read. *Music by Faden's Band. Donations accepted for storm damage. $1.00 per raffle ticket. Win a set of Mr. Jones' Rocking chairs.*

The children had also enticed the older crowd by inviting members of the community to set up a multi-family yard sale. Sebastian was still feeling skeptical that the event would raise enough money to make a difference. Eva suggested they all consider getting jobs, which struck him as a good idea, until he remembered that he'd be eighteen soon and would probably have to find a fulltime job anyway—and a new home. His chest tightened at the thought.

"What's he looking at?" Tommie asked.

Sebastian followed her glance, and it landed on Roy Simms, leaning against the entrance of Ken's Laundromat. His eyes were on them.

"That kid's trouble," Sebastian said softly. "You stay away from him."

"That won't be a problem."

***

EVA RAISED HERSELF from her knees and brushed the creases from her bed cover, before placing her rosary beads back in her music box. The heat in the bedroom was becoming unbearable, so she made her way downstairs to the kitchen for a glass of water.

She found Tommie standing at the kitchen table staring with a baffled expression at the two playing cards she held in each hand. The rest of the deck was spread out chaotically in front of her. Eva went to the sink, but jumped back instinctively, letting out a soft squeal when something moved in the basin. She rose onto her toes and peered in.

"Tommie! Why is there a turtle in the sink?"

"It's for my trick," Tommie answered, without looking at her. "Don't touch it."

"Wasn't planning on it," she mumbled and wrinkled her nose in disgust. She sighed heavily. She'd woken up that morning feeling agitated and afraid. And even after her morning devotional and praying a full rosary, the feeling still hadn't left her. She stepped out into the backyard.

It was a beautiful day, without a single cloud obstructing the deep blue sky, but even that couldn't lift her mood. She recognized Benedict's leg swinging from the deck of the treehouse and walked closer.

"Hey, Benedict? What's going on?"

He sat up, holding a notepad and a pencil. "Thinking up jokes." He scratched his head with his pencil. "But for some reason, I'm not as funny on paper."

She put on an exaggerated, sad face, pushing her bottom lip out, so Benedict could see that she was sympathetic to his plight, but he just rolled his eyes, groaned loudly, and lay down again.

"Who thought of a dumb variety show anyway?"

It wasn't me, she thought sadly.

Ahead of her, in the next field, she noticed Sebastian practicing his lassoing. Faden was with him. She sighed again. *Lord, please ease this feeling*, she prayed as she walked toward the barn. The horses were grazing, so it was empty.

She began humming to herself while she walked slowly up the center aisle of the barn, running her hand along the top of each stall door she passed.

"There can be miracles," she began to sing, and then hummed a little louder. She liked the way the sound of her voice echoed in the enclosed area. When she reached the center of the barn, she walked aimlessly around the tack and feed area, tapping her fingers along the tackle and turning in slow circles. She was losing herself in the moment and it felt freeing.

She headed back up the aisle toward the entrance. "When you believe, somehow you will," she sang louder and more confident. "You will when you believe."

She turned slowly again, but suddenly jumped at the sight of Mr. Jones, who was standing at the barn entrance watching her.

"Don't let me stop you, Eva, I was enjoying that."

"Oh, Mr. Jones." Her face flushed. "I was just taking a walk."

"Are you going to sing at the variety show?" He turned on the hose and washed dry mud off a horseshoe.

"Oh, no. I only like to sing in church." The feeling in Eva's chest tightened again.

Mr. Jones smiled and nodded. "That seems a shame. It'd be worth a ticket just to hear you sing."

"Really?" She smiled. "I think it's best to save the singing for church."

He nodded.

"Don't you think . . . ?" she added the question casually.

Mr. Jones shook the water from the horseshoe and smiled. "I think if you have a beautiful voice, you should share it with everyone . . . assuming you enjoy singing."

She smiled and shrugged, but didn't say anything.

"Eva," he said. "Your voice is your own. Trust in yourself and the gifts that God has blessed you with. Use them to glorify Him, and you will succeed."

"But, Mr. Jones, it could also lead to destruction." Only after she said the words did she realize that it sounded a little nuts. Maybe she was nuts, because she believed it to be true.

"Do you really feel that way?"

"It's happened before," she whispered.

Mr. Jones smiled and shook his head, adding, "I thought you had the most faith."

***

ONE EVENING WHEN Martha walked into the kitchen, she found Sebastian sitting alone at the large table with a full glass of milk next to him. Only the light from the stove illuminated the space, but Martha could see that his shoulders were slouched forward and his head was bowed. As she stood gazing sadly at him, she remembered David mentioning that Sebastian had seemed depressed or concerned about something recently. She had told her husband that she'd try and take a moment with the boy, but she had been distracted by the recent worries that had slowly consumed all their lives. A feeling of shame surged through her.

"My sweet Sabe." She walked up to him. The boy's head jolted, as if she'd woken him from deep thought, and she leaned over to kiss him on the head. "I remember the first night you came here. You couldn't sleep without your iced milk."

He raised his glass, took a sip, and tilted the glass so the ice clinked for effect.

She went to the fridge and poured herself a glass. When she was sitting opposite him, she saw that he was avoiding eye contact.

"Sebastian?"

Reluctantly, he looked up at her and she saw his watery eyes staring back at her.

"Honey, what is it?"

He shrugged, then said, "I know things don't stay the same forever." He paused. "I guess I just wish they would."

"In what way?" It was no surprise if the children sensed the tension in the house, when she herself was having a hard time keeping it together.

Sebastian took a deep breath. "I understand that we're not your real kids, and when it's time, we'll have to leave. I mean, how could you want us when our own parents didn't?"

"Sebastian," she said firmly.

"I understand, Martha. Babies, toddlers, they're all cute, but then we grow up."

"You cut that out right now, Sebastian." She was more hurt than angry. "I'm not your father."

He stopped suddenly and looked at her, surprised.

She bit her lip. She knew that Sebastian and his father had fought all the time. It was part of the "client file" that they received on each child. After losing his wife at a young age, Sebastian's father also lost both his enthusiasm for life and for his child. While once Sebastian had been the jewel in the couple's world, he had become a reminder to his father of what he had lost. So, to soften the edges, the memories, and the long days without his wife, his father had resorted to drinking as often as he could. His devotion to the bottle eventually lost him his job, then the family home, and consequently the respect of his son.

She knew how hard it must have been for Sebastian to watch his once successful father throw his life away, and to feel their relationship disintegrate from bickering to arguing, and then eventually from arguing to physical fighting.

They had fought often, they had fought long, and they had fought hard, until finally a school nurse could no longer ignore Sebastian's bruises. Even after he had been warned by authorities, and his son had been put under supervision, Sebastian's father had continued to drink, until he finally was arrested for driving while intoxicated. After choosing to argue his case with the arresting officer using his fists, he was jailed. Martha thought, though, that Sebastian had come to feel secure since coming to live at Sunshine Ranch.

"What has gotten into you, Sabe?"

"I don't want to leave, Martha." He looked at her urgently. "I don't ever want to leave, but I know I have to."

She sat across from him and reached for his hand. "Sabe. My sweet Sabe, I'd have you live with us forever if I could, but that would be selfish of me."

Sebastian looked at her confused.

"Because the world deserves a part of you, and you deserve the world."

"I don't want the world. I just want Sunshine Ranch—you, David, everyone, just as they are. Even Benedict."

"Oh, Sabe," she said softly. "Whatever you decide, we will all be with you. I just wish for you an amazing life. I want you to explore this world, live out your full potential, utilize the gifts that God blessed you with, and do your part in making this world a better place."

His forehead crinkled with worry. "That's a lot of stuff."

"Yes. Yes it is. But nothing is impossible with God. People do it every day in their own unique way. And unless you experience this world, unless you work hard, love deep, and overcome life's challenges—unless you experience *life*, you will never really know complete happiness. Of course," she added after a short pause, "If you decide to stay with us forever, then that'd work just as well for me."

***

ON THE MORNING of the Credence Variety Show, Tommie helped Eva, Micah, and Benedict unfold chairs and set them up to create a crescent-shaped seating area in the corral as Mr. Jones, David, and Sebastian put the final touches to the stage.

At that moment, they all heard the sound of a car revving its engine and peeling out at the front of the house. A few seconds later, Roy's white Ford Fiesta sped up the drive, and Faden appeared from the front of the house. They watched as he ran toward them. His face was flushed and he was breathing heavily, clutching a wad of orange paper.

"What's going on?" Eva asked, as he neared them.

"Roy," Faden said angrily, and he held the paper toward them. "He just gave me these before bailing out of here."

Tommie saw that the papers were actually the posters that they'd put up around town. Faden explained that Roy had pulled them all down the day they had posted them and held onto them until today.

"So, no one even knows about the show?" Tommie asked. "What is your brother's problem?"

David, Sebastian, and Mr. Jones joined the group.

Eva rested her hands on her hips. "Great, no one's even going to show."

"Yes, they will," David said. "We've all been talking about this in town. Word of mouth will bring them here."

"Yeah, but not enough of them," Sebastian said in a low voice.

"It'll be fine," David said.

"Look," Mr. Jones pointed up at the drive where two

cars were arriving. "Betty Carter and Mavis Flanagan are here. They're setting up part of the yard sale. I'm sure they've spread the word."

"It's not going to be enough." Tommie was urgent and close to tears.

"It'll be fine," David said sternly. "Now you guys go get ready. Go on. We'll take care of things here."

And that was it. They would get ready, and then they would pray that enough word had been spread around town. If not, they'd never make enough cash to deem the event worthwhile.

***

EVA WATCHED AS Tommie rushed around the room in a robe, tripping over clothes, shoes, and books that lay in her path. She opened her closet door and surveyed its disorganized contents through wet tousled hair. After a moment, she pulled out a black shirt, glanced disapprovingly at it and threw it over her shoulder. A few more items flew through the air before a shirt met her approval.

"Oh, man." She tried to scratch off a permanent stain of what seemed to be pasta sauce. "Great." It was the next to fly.

Eva continued to watch discreetly, without a word. She knew Tommie was in no mood to be interfered with.

Tommie turned back to the closet and searched its contents again, and then she turned back and scanned the room, obviously looking for something specific. She dropped to her knees and looked under the bed.

"Ah ha!" She pulled out her long black dress and slipped it on, trying to smooth the wrinkles with her hand. She grabbed a brush and began pulling it through her wet hair. "Ow, ow," she whined as each stroke pulled at the knots.

Eva winced, feeling each tug. She wanted to jump up and help her, but knew that Tommie would get mad and accuse her of being superior, or something equally ridiculous.

"Stupid hair," she said quietly as she tugged at the brush. "Stupid hair, stupid hair."

She looked at her reflection and the matted mess she had created and she gritted her teeth, then resumed yanking and tugging at it.

Finally, Eva just couldn't take any more. She jumped from her bed, ran over to Tommie, and grabbed the brush.

"Let me *help* you," Eva said, more aggressively than she had intended.

"*No!*" Tommie yelled, but she didn't fight to get the brush back. She just stood facing her pitiful image as Eva began brushing out the knots.

Tommie glared at her in the mirror. "Why do you do everything so much better than *everyone?*" she said with a sneer.

"What?" Eva rolled her eyes and caught Tommie's gaze in the mirror.

"You just . . . *do* things better; *look* better . . . everything comes so *easily*—"

"What are you talking about?" Eva was getting angry.

The other girl shrugged and looked down. "Forget it."

Eva resumed brushing, and for a moment there was silence, but she knew that it was time to make one thing clear.

11

EVA TOOK A DEEP breath. "There's one memory that I let myself think about, just so I can remember my blessings."

She continued carefully to brush the knots out of Tommie's hair, while Tommie watched her in the mirror.

"My seventh birthday party. My mom was a singer, but I guess she liked drinking more." She swallowed hard. She hadn't told anyone about her mother and she didn't want to get emotional or she'd never make her point.

"I could never figure out her moods, y'know? One minute she'd be angry, next she'd be happy, and then, for no reason, she'd be mad again." She and Tommie exchanged a look. "So that day, while this big, fancy party was being set up, I remember feeling a pain here." She pointed to her chest with the brush. "But I promised God I'd be perfect for her. And so when everyone got there, she wanted to sing me a birthday song and make a huge deal out of it."

She brushed absently as she visualized the day clearly in her mind. "I was wearing my white chiffon dress with a pink satin ribbon around my waist, and I was wearing these cute silver shoes. I watched my mom hold herself up with the microphone stand, and she kept forgetting her words. It was awful, and I remember thinking, where's my mom gone? I can still feel my face smiling, even though I wanted to cry."

"And when I looked around, everyone was pretending to be impressed. Then this lady came up to me to wish me a happy birthday, and I said 'thank you,' and that was it. But all of a sudden, my mother stopped singing." She paused and returned Tommie's gaze in the mirror, her eyes wide with the pain of the memory. "Right in the middle of her song. Then she yells, 'You're not even listening, Eva.' Her words were all slurry. 'You ungrateful child. After all this.' And she pointed around her and I could hear people gasping all around me, like, oh, here it comes. I'll never forget it—she charged toward me and then . . . falls flat on her face. My party was over."

Tommie didn't respond. Eva continued to brush her hair and muttered softly, "That's just *one* memory. It's not the best and it's not the worst."

"Was she okay?"

"Oh, yeah, she was fine." And she paused again before adding, "Until she decided to burn our house down and they sent her to the nuthouse."

She sat on the bed. "My grandparents didn't even want me."

She remembered how they had been contacted immediately, but they had insisted that they really could not disrupt their retirement by taking on their granddaughter full time. After all, they had done their part with "the girl's mother." So, Eva had found herself at Sunshine Ranch within the month.

She prayed every night that her mother would be better soon, but she never once asked God for them to resume their life together, even without the crazy parts, because she wasn't sure she could ever be good enough.

She pulled herself out of her thoughts. "If I was *so perfect*, then why am I here? Why would no one want me? Huh? There'd be a line out the door, wouldn't there?"

She stood up and resumed brushing. "We all have our issues, Tommie. We are *all* rejects in some way or another."

"No, you are *not!*"

They both turned and saw David, Sebastian, Benedict, and Micah all standing in the doorway.

"None of you are rejects, and that's *not* why you're here," David said and walked over to the girls. "Don't you ever think that you are here because there's something *wrong* with you."

"Then why are we here?" she asked.

"You are here . . ." he began to say, then seemed to take a moment to consider his words before resuming again. "You are here because God sent you to me."

"Oh, David!" Benedict was about to walk away.

"It's true." David looked back at the boys. "Your mothers and fathers, for some reason or another, couldn't do it right."

"Do what right?" Tommie asked.

"Take care of you . . . they just didn't have it in them. They weren't strong enough."

"Smart enough," Tommie muttered.

"Sober enough," Sebastian said.

"Stop," David said gently. "Don't do that."

"Don't do what? Be mad at them?" Benedict's face reddened.

"No—no, you can be mad at them," David said. "You can be mad all you want, but at some point, you need to let it go. You need to tell yourself that it doesn't matter anymore. You need to forgive them for what they did and did not do, and you need to move on."

"What if I can't do that?" Tommie asked.

David thought a moment before answering. "If you can't forgive and move on, then your feelings will grow and fester, and they will eat you alive."

Tommie rolled her eyes. "Whatever."

"They will. I'm serious. They will take over your lives and they will distract you from doing, and being, the best you can do and be. They will rob you of your potential, because you'll be so full of anger and resentment. And then, if you meet someone and have babies of your own, you'll pass on the feelings you stored inside of you for so long, when what you really need to do is start fresh. Give your family and your children a chance to live a full and clean life. You don't want *them* to pay. *Do* you?"

"No," some of them answered.

"No, you want to give them what you should have had, and you want them to give you what you always yearned for . . . finally. A wonderful home and family life."

After a brief silence, as the children thought about his words, Benedict asked, "Is that even possible?"

"You can do all things through Christ who strengthens you," David said.

Benedict shook his head.

***

IT WAS A SLOW START to the day's events, and Tommie continued to stress over the small donation amounts that were coming in. She didn't want the success of the event to be measured by the cash they received, but the reality was that their future at Sunshine Ranch depended on it. She stood with Micah and Mr. Jones behind a folding table between the corral and the house as they greeted the guests. Mr. Jones accepted the money with a nod and a smile, before stuffing it into a box wrapped in brown paper. He chatted briefly with each guest, because he knew them all well.

Finally, to Tommie's relief, more cars descended the drive, one behind the other. Sebastian and Benedict had set up signs directing them all to park on the other side of the house. Suddenly, their biggest concern was not whether there would be enough people, but whether they would have enough food to feed them.

Miss Madden clutched her music sheets to her chest and watched guests taking their seats.

"How exciting this all is." She looked at the blue sky. "And the Lord has blessed us with a perfect day."

Fr. Thaddeus nodded and took another gulp of his cherry lemonade. The sun was shining, but a cool breeze swept over the guests, providing relief from the heat as they sat waiting for the show to start.

The show began with Sebastian's lassoing demonstration. He stood in the center of the stage, wearing brown leather chaps and a matching cowboy hat, lent to him by Faden. He proudly executed the tricks that David had taught him and ended his performance by jumping off the stage and striding down the center aisle while twirling the lasso overhead. When he reached the end of the aisle, he threw out the loop just as Faden galloped past on Captain Jack. The lasso dropped over him and tightened around his shoulders, and Sebastian pulled him off the back of the horse.

The audience gasped, but the boys had practiced extensively, so Faden's maneuver was more of a lunge than a fall from the back of the horse, and he landed on his feet. The crowd cheered. Sebastian called to the horse, and it stopped immediately and waited for Faden to retrieve him. The guests were impressed, not just by the boys' performance, but also by the obedient horse, which had been an untamed brute when it arrived at the ranch months before.

Next came Benedict's stand-up comedy act, a routine based on the Credence siblings. He called his theme "Bathroom Tales," and made the audience laugh with impressions of Eva and Tommie fighting over the bathroom.

He shook his head. "It's a never-ending battle when you have to share a bathroom with a girl. Especially *our* girls."

He was nervous when he first took the stage, but now the audience was laughing, and that was all he wanted. He put on an exaggerated expression of exhaustion that made the audience laugh louder.

"I'm telling you, you need a timer and reservations or you won't get a shower in for *months*."

He ended his act with an anecdote about Melanie and Francine running around the house in nothing but suds, while the whole Credence family chased them from all directions.

Nana Credence laughed uncontrollably and nudged the person next to her. "That's a true story," she said giggling. "That's really what happened."

When it was Isabella's turn to dance, Miss Madden took her seat at the piano, with Micah standing next to her, along with Faden and his guitar.

Isabella climbed the stage from the left side and stood front and center. She wore a pink leotard with a knee-length tutu, which she smoothed with both hands as she waited for the music to start. Miss Madden began to play, and Isabella replied with a curtsey. Faden sang the words to

Chris Tomlin's "I will Rise," while Micah and Miss Madden joined in the chorus, as Isabella turned a few times, reaching her arms out in ballet fashion, and swayed with the music.

Nana Credence had helped her with her choreography. Although neither had any ballet or jazz experience—and Isabella was far from a professional dancer—the audience watched in admiration at a child who put her heart and soul into her performance.

Martha stood on the sidelines with her hands clutched in front of her mouth. David came up behind her and wrapped his arms around her waist.

"She's beautiful," he murmured, and Martha could only nod.

Eva was amazed that Isabella didn't look afraid at all. She was equally impressed with Micah's singing. When they were finished, the audience cheered and whistled, and a gleaming Isabella descended the stage and ran into Nana Credence's waiting arms.

Martha and David were next with their version of Lee Ann Womack's "I Hope You Dance," which they dedicated to their children. Their act was a last minute decision, encouraged by David, who told Martha that they owed it to the children to participate. Martha laughed through most of the song, and David kept forgetting the words, looking to Miss Madden for prompting. They sang completely out of tune, with Martha at a much higher pitch than David, but everyone loved it.

Tommie's magic show was the most entertaining for everyone. Micah, Melanie, and Francine were her assistants. The little ones were dressed in clown outfits and Micah sported a top hat and tails. Tommie wore a gold cloak over her black dress—which Eva had insisted she iron.

The act began as planned, with Tommie performing a quick vanishing card trick. Micah promptly replaced one set of items with another, and Tommie followed her first act with the stand-up trick.

The young members of the audience watched in fascination and gasped in all the right places. But as perfectly as the show commenced, it quickly began to fall apart. After the hanky trick, Francine stood center stage with her finger up her nose. Then, before Tommie got to the rabbit-out-of-the-hat trick, Melanie picked up the hat from the edge of the stage and screamed when she pulled out the stuffed bunny. Tommie didn't mind that the audience laughed. She couldn't hold it in a few times herself.

"What happened to the turtle?" Nana Credence asked Sebastian in between her own hoots of laughter.

"It escaped." The two of them laughed uproariously.

Micah tried to keep order, but ended up chasing both the giggling girls around Tommie, who tried to ignore the commotion and maintain a "show must go on" attitude.

Eva watched as the act slowly crumbled, yet her foster sister just stifled a laugh. It moved Eva to see how all her foster siblings were doing their part to pitch in and help save the house. But something was missing.

While both Tommie and Micah dragged the girls off the stage—Melanie with a lopsided clown nose and Francine with her head lost in Micah's top hat—while the audience stood laughing and clapping, Eva approached Miss Madden and whispered in her ear.

Tommie's being the last act on the program, the guests now stood and prepared to go to the barbecue, until a tinkle of piano keys caught their attention. Eva was now center stage.

She held the microphone in both hands and waited nervously while Miss Madden played the introduction to "When You Believe," from *The Prince of Egypt*. Eva began to sing a little unsteady, her head so low that no one could see her face, but as she continued, she raised her chin, and her voice became smooth and rang out into the air.

It was a beautiful sound and the guests watched her in wonder, unable to pull their gaze away from her face. She sang on into the blue sky. She sang to the sun and she sang to the Lord, and when the song came to an end, there was complete silence. Eva waited, afraid that she had sung in completely the wrong key, but then all of a sudden a loud eruption of applause and cheers filled the air.

The children crowded her as she descended the stage steps. Their words were lost as they talked excitedly over each other. Martha and David hugged her and kissed her head. Nana Credence nodded approvingly while she bounced a sleeping Peachie, afraid she'd cry if she spoke.

Mr. Jones also hugged her and then in her ear he whispered, "You have been blessed."

On the stage, Faden and his band began setting up. Sebastian, Tommie, Micah, and Benedict started moving the folding chairs to the tables near the food area, and clearing a dance floor in front of the stage.

"Hey, Micah, wait up." Benedict quickened his steps, carrying two folded chairs over each shoulder.

Micah waited for him to catch up, his chairs in the same position, and the two of them rushed off. Sebastian shook his head and smiled.

David and Mr. Jones manned the ribs and chicken on the barbecue. Miss Milly had donated a delicious selection of salads, which she now helped Eva and Martha put out for the guests. A line began to form, and people started helping themselves to the food. It wasn't long before the band was ready and country music filled the air.

"I *love* this song," Eva said, grinning, and then began to sing along. She popped a lid off a salad and stuck a plastic serving spoon into it. "*God is great, beer is good, and people are crazy* . . ." She was in a joyous mood. It was a perfect day so far. She'd been so afraid of singing outside of church, but it had felt right.

Looking around, she guessed that there must be at least three hundred people there, and with most of them donating more than five bucks a piece. *That's a fortune.* On top of that, they'd sold a lot of raffle tickets. Mr. Jones had made a matching pair of sun chairs for the prize and had carved a radiant sun in their headrests. The prize also came with a promise that he'd carve the names of the winners on the back of each, so everyone was eager to win. Eva walked over to the beverage table and Sebastian came to stand next to her.

"I'm so proud of you, Eva," he said sincerely. "I know how hard it must've been for you to get up there and sing."

"Thanks."

***

As Sebastian helped himself to another cup of lemonade, he noticed a man watching him from a short distance away. He squinted to get a better look and, when he did, his hand released the cup so that it fell to the ground, spilling the contents on Eva's foot.

"Hey!" She began to protest, but Sebastian's expression prompted her to follow his gaze. The man suddenly turned and walked swiftly toward the parked cars.

Sebastian's heart beat against his chest. He didn't know what to do at first, but he knew he couldn't let the man leave without finding out what he wanted. So he rushed after him, shouting, "Hey. *Hey!*"

As he got closer, the man suddenly stopped. Sebastian stopped also.

12

"WHY ARE YOU HERE?" Sebastian called after him.

His father had heard him despite the loud music and now turned slowly to face him, staring silently for a moment before saying, "I needed to see you."

"Why?"

"I have things I need to say to you."

"Well, I have nothing to say to you." Sebastian immediately asked God to forgive his lie.

"That's fine, because I need you to listen."

As his father walked toward him, Sebastian stepped backed.

"Being in prison affords you a lot of time to relive your mistakes."

"I wouldn't know."

His father nodded. "You have every right to be angry at me. That's why I'm here." He slouched as he stood there, far from the tall proud man Sebastian remembered as a child. "I have to tell you that I'm sorry, Sebastian. When your mother died, a part of me died inside." His voice cracked.

Sebastian felt a lump rise in his throat and tried to swallow. It was difficult hearing about his mother after so many years, especially from his father's lips.

"She was an amazing woman."

"I know."

His father nodded. "Of course you do. For some time, I forgot that you knew that. And I forgot that you were loved by her as well. I wasn't the only one who lost her." Tears fell down the man's cheeks and he wiped them away. "I'm sorry for that."

Sebastian didn't know what to say. If he said anything, he would break down, too, something he didn't want to do in front of this man.

His father tried to compose his emotions. "I still miss her. I still think about her."

"I was still here. She was my mother. I loved her too," Sebastian shouted over the music.

"I know. I know that now. But when I was drinking, I never thought about anyone else. It was all about me, and that was all that mattered." His father looked at him, as if seeing him for the first time. "I hurt you. Your mother would have been disgusted with my behavior, just as I am whenever I look back at how I treated you. She never would have forgiven me."

Sebastian saw the pain in his father's eyes.

"But I'm hoping you will. You deserve a happiness that I'm not sure I can give you anymore."

"I don't need you to make me happy. I gave up on that a long time ago."

The music ended. When he looked around, he noticed that Eva, Martha, and David were watching him from a short distance. *Waiting for what?* But he knew they were giving him what he needed, again.

"I'm seeing someone," his father said. "A shrink!" He

laughed and walked cautiously toward him. "I had a great life . . . *we* had a great life. I should never have allowed it to fall apart after your mother died . . . because it cost me the other best thing I had . . . *you*." He spoke quickly, choking on the last word. "But I did. And I can never take that time back. I can never forget it, nor will I *ever* forget it. It's done."

He was standing in front of Sebastian now. "I don't think there's any way I can make up for it."

"No. You can't."

"But I did need to tell you this, and I hope in some way it eases your mind to know that I never blamed you."

A lump rose in Sebastian's throat again.

"I never blamed you. I never *hated* you. You just reminded me of her so much. You *are* her. And even now. . . ." He searched his son's face. "I see her in you. Come here." He pulled Sebastian into his arms.

Sebastian tried to shove him away, but then allowed himself a small moment of comfort in his arms.

"I love you, Sebastian."

Sebastian suddenly felt a knot within him loosen. All he had ever really wanted was to hear those words. He felt his father sobbing into his shoulder and waited another second before pushing him away.

"I'm sorry," the man whispered. He kissed his son on the forehead and held him at arm's length for a moment, gazing at his face as he shook his head in clear admiration.

Sebastian couldn't remember the last time his father had looked at him that way, but he knew it had been before his mother died.

Finally, his father released him and turned to go. Sebastian watched him walk away, his heart still beating fast. Then the man stopped and turned back to him.

"I hope that I can check in on you, now and then?"

Sebastian nodded.

His father smiled and once again turned away; again he took only a few steps before turning back to his boy.

"You are happy aren't you, son?"

Sebastian's heart jumped at that word. "Yes." His lip trembled. "I'm *very* happy," he said in a shaky voice.

"Good." His father nodded, and then turned away for the last time. "Good."

***

THE DAY WAS COMING to an end as Tommie watched Martha and David dancing a slow dance in a sea of satisfied guests. They held each other close while glancing at their family members dotted around them. On the outskirts of the dance floor, Tommie noticed Benedict introducing Micah to some of his friends. Miss Madden was exceptionally happy, since she had won the raffle, and Mr. Jones' chairs. Eva danced with Melanie in her arms, and the child giggled and clung on tight with every dip and turn. Isabella sat feeding Francine pieces of cut fruit, and Nana Credence was in deep conversation with Mr. Jones.

Tommie's eyes were on Faden now, who strummed the end of Garth Brooks' "More Than a Memory" on his guitar, bobbing his head to the music. Her stomach tightened as she watched him. It was getting harder and harder every day to be around him. She hated that feeling, especially since she enjoyed helping David with the horses and Faden was always there.

She looked down at the yellow dress that Eva had insisted she change into after the show, and wished she hadn't listened to her. She felt ridiculous out of her usual black and decided to go inside and change. As she walked away slowly, feigning smiles at those she passed, she tried not to feel so upset. *It has been a great day,* she thought, *and I should be grateful for that and not so selfish. We may have saved the ranch today.* She pushed Faden out of her mind and looked around her. She hadn't expected the event to last this long, but it seemed no one wanted to leave. There was an hour or so of sunlight left, so she decided that she would change out of the yellow dress, come back, and celebrate with her foster siblings.

"Tommie!"

Faden's voice made her heart jump. She turned, telling herself to remain calm.

"Where you going?"

"Inside." She shrugged, hoping he couldn't see her face change color as she felt it flush.

He caught up to her and they walked side by side toward the house. "Why?"

"I want to change."

"Why?"

She smirked. "Because I look ridiculous."

He looked her up and down. "Turn around."

"No." She smiled shyly.

"Go on, do a spin. Let me see."

"I will *not.*" She tried to hold back from laughing.

"Well, I can't give you my honest opinion until I see the full picture."

"I don't *need* your opinion, thank you very much."

"Well, fine, then I'll have to agree with you that you look ridiculous." She pushed him playfully. They were nearing the kitchen door. "Hey, you want to take a ride?"

"Aren't you supposed to be playing right now?" She nodded toward the band.

"They kicked me out. Said I couldn't play a note."

"You're crazy." She laughed. "You sounded amazing."

"You want to ride for a while or what?"

"Let me change first."

"Yeah, please. You look ridiculous. I'll saddle up."
She pushed him again.

They were quiet as they rode toward the lake. She hated the awkwardness that seemed to surround them the last few times they'd been together. Her stomach was tight, and she wondered if he could sense her anxiety.

"You alright?" he asked suddenly.

She shrugged. "Yeah, why?"

"You're acting weird."

"No, I'm not."

"You really are." They had reached the lake behind the house and Faden climbed down, clicking his tongue for the horse to move by a tree, where he tied her. He hung his hat on the saddle.

Tommie followed his lead and stood next to him beside the water. They gazed silently ahead at the panorama that filled the horizon before them. The sun was slowly descending toward the water, and the sky blazed with a spectacular mix of orange and red. She closed her eyes and took a long, calming breath, then sat down.

"You know, I think we should probably head back." Faden walked toward his horse.

"What?" She stood, confused. "What're you doing?"

He turned to her. "What am I doing? Well, actually, I'm not sure." His hair fell into his face and he brushed it away casually. "What I *wanted* to do was bring you here, sit quietly watching this amazing view, and break it to you that I really like you . . . a *lot* . . . but now I'm afraid. I'm afraid you don't feel the same way and I'll end up looking like a real idiot, and you know, I don't think I want that."

For a second she felt herself stop breathing, and then she gasped for air. She wanted to tell him that she liked him also, but she didn't know how to say it in a way that wouldn't sound silly. *And what if I faint?* She may have been standing there a little too long juggling her thoughts because he shrugged and turned back to his horse.

"Faden, wait." She rushed toward him. "Please wait."

"Wait for what? For you to tell me that you like me too, but not in that way? And why can't we just be friends?" He turned to her with a pained expression.

"No." She walked toward him. "Wait for me to tell you that I like you too." She stood in front of him. "And in the same way that you like me, I think."

They stared at each other for a few seconds before he smiled. "Really?"

"Really." She smiled warily.

"Well, then. . . ." He scratched his chin. "In that case, I'll stay."

"Good."

They went back to sitting beside the water. The awkwardness had returned at a much higher level, but the inevitable had to happen, and so Faden finally turned to her and asked simply, "Can I just kiss you now?"

She laughed. "I thought you were a good Christian boy."

"Oh, I am." He lifted his left hand and tapped the silver ring on his finger with his thumb. "Pure and proud."

He grinned. "So don't get fresh." She laughed again before he leaned in and pressed a kiss onto her lips.

***

EVA REVIEWED THE PAPER in front of her, glanced at the piles of cash, and nodded with satisfaction. "Nearly three thousand dollars."

"Are you kidding me?" Sebastian beamed.

The children sat on the floor of the great room. Neat piles of fives, tens, and twenties were lined up alongside quarters, dimes, and nickels.

"That's amazing," Tommie added.

"Yeah, but is it enough?" Eva crinkled her brow.

"It's *tons*," said Benedict.

At that moment, Martha walked into the room, wiping her hands with a towel. "How did you guys do?"

"We made nearly three thousand dollars," Micah said, wide-eyed.

"Wow. That's pretty impressive," she said slowly. "You guys are so amazing."

"Is it enough?" Eva asked.

She nodded. "Well, it's definitely a good amount of money."

David entered the room and whistled at the sight of the money. "Ooh whee . . . you did well." He smiled and sat down.

"Is it enough to keep the house?" Tommie asked.

"You guys—" Martha began nervously.

"Will this money help save the house?" Isabella insisted.

David cleared his throat and looked seriously at them. "You children shouldn't be worrying about that business."

"But will it help?" Tommie repeated.

"*Every* penny helps," David said in a low voice, but he didn't convince anyone. Martha was looking at the floor.

Eva knew something was wrong now. "But will we get to keep the house?"

"No. No it's not enough to keep the house." David said finally and shrugged.

"We can have more shows," Isabella said.

"No." David stood up. "No. This was a wonderful, kind, amazing thing that you all did, but it won't save Sunshine Ranch."

13

TOMMIE THREW HER HANDS in the air in despair. "You mean we did that for *nothing*?"

"You didn't do it for nothing. You all came together like brothers and sisters," Martha said.

"Yeah, but it's not going to keep us together like brothers and sisters, is it?" Isabella said softly.

"I'll get a job," was all Sebastian could say.

"Me too," Eva interjected. "We can make this work."

"Benedict, are you okay?" Martha asked.

"I knew I'd be moving again. I just *knew* it."

"Oh, Benedict, please." Martha covered her mouth with her hands.

"But you told me I wouldn't." He looked directly at her. "You said I'd found my home, but you lied, just like the rest of them." His eyes narrowed in accusation.

"Benny, we never lied," Martha said softly. "We never once believed that you'd leave us, and we're still working on keeping us all together, even if we can't keep the house."

"Yeah, but there's no guarantee, is there?" Tommie asked.

"Nothing's guaranteed," David said.

"They're going to take me to some awful place again." Benedict's voice was shaking. "And just when I get used to that awfulness, they'll take me to another place, and—"

"*Stop it.*" Martha rushed over to him and pulled him toward her. "They will *not.* They will not. We will *fix* this. I *promise.*"

Benedict pulled away from her forcefully. "You promised before, but it turned out to be a *lie.*"

"Benny, don't say mean things," Eva yelled.

"Why not? I'm the mean one, remember? I *always* say the *meanest* things." His anger took them all by surprise.

"Benny, you have to have faith," Martha said weakly.

"Stop saying that. *Stop saying that.* Faith hasn't helped us." He threw his arms up in frustration. "Faith didn't stop Micah from being sick. Faith didn't stop us from losing this house. And faith *won't* keep us together."

Isabella was crying now, so Sebastian put his arm around her, while Tommie stood watching in silence. Eva looked at Martha and David, waiting for their answer, because she too needed to hear it.

"Faith is all we have in times like this, Benny," David said. "Nobody knows what life's going to hand us, but if we have God on our side, it'll all work out."

"I don't believe it." Benedict was suddenly composed. "I never will." He walked out of the room, leaving the others in silence, but for Isabella's sobbing.

***

MICAH WATCHED BENEDICT'S silhouette, rigid and upright as he sat sleepless in the darkness.

He wanted to reassure his new friend, but knew that any mention of God would only make Benedict angrier. Just like Martha and David, Micah always looked to God. He watched as long as he could, hoping Benedict would talk to him first, but his patience was in vain. Eventually, he couldn't keep his eyes open.

When he woke up later, it was still dark, but the silhouette was gone. He climbed out of bed and went to Benedict's bed, whispering his name as he tipped-toed over. But the bed was empty.

He heard a squeak—the same sound that must have woken him up. He rushed to the hall and saw two shadows disappear at the bottom of the stairs. He dashed back to his room to put his clothes on. As he pulled on his jeans, he stumbled over to the window and saw the shadows move quickly away from the house.

Outside in the darkness, Micah felt a surprising chill in the air. He hurried over to the treehouse and looked up at it, expecting to find them there. But something was wrong—there was no light or sound of muffled voices. Then he saw movement in the distance, and he started toward it, careful not to push himself in his frail condition. But he would never catch up at such a slow speed. He stopped.

"Benny," he called out as softly as he could, but the shadows kept moving.

"*Benny*," he yelled louder. The shadows stopped and Micah jogged to catch up. As he got closer, they rushed toward him, and he saw then that the other shadow with Benedict was Tommie.

"What are you doing? What are you *doing?*" Benedict asked angrily.

"What are *you* doing?" Micah tried to relax his breathing. He didn't really need to ask. The backpacks they carried told the whole story.

"Never you mind."

"Micah, you need to go back," Tommie said gently.

"If you guys go, *I'm* going." Micah had no idea why he

had said that—he hadn't even realized that they were leaving until just now. But he felt as if he had no choice. *What else am I going to do? Go back to the house and sound the alarm? Then Benedict and Tommie would never talk to me again. No, I have to talk them out of this,* he thought.

"You can't come," Tommie said sternly. "You're too sick."

"I'm not going back without you guys."

"Why? You have *faith*," Benedict mocked.

"Cut it out, Benny. Micah, you can't come, but I can't stop you, and we have to go." Tommie walked off.

Benedict followed, and then Micah. They trudged through the field in silence for a few minutes, with only the sound of their steps dragging through the long grass and two competing frogs croaking nearby.

Micah was the first to break the peace by asking, "Where're we going?" He was worried. To God, he prayed for the words that would talk both of them out of this decision, and he prayed that those words would come soon. Time was running out. He had to get them back to the house before they trekked too far. And it was getting so cold.

***

TOMMIE HAD MADE A PLAN. She'd developed it years ago when she had first arrived at the ranch, in the event that this foster home turned out to be a disaster. When she thought back to that time in her life, she felt sorry that she was actually living out her plan, even though she loved Martha and David.

"I figured we could make our way to the bus station and head across the country."

"Where to?" Micah interrupted her thoughts.

"I don't know," she said, "We can figure that out later. Right now we have to leave before someone figures out we're gone."

"The bus station is miles away."

They walked for about five minutes more before reaching the lake. Micah suggested that they take a break, but Benedict wasn't happy, telling them that if they kept taking breaks, they wouldn't get anywhere. Tommie agreed with Micah and sat next to him on a large rock facing the water.

The full moon shone on the surface of the water. Tommie listened to the gentle lapping, and her thoughts wandered to Faden. Bubbles popped in her stomach as she remembered their brief kiss and his hand holding hers while they looked out at the same water, not so long ago. Her heart sank, because she was leaving him too, but she had no choice, she reasoned. If she was sent somewhere else, she wouldn't be able to see him anyway. At least, this way, she could decide where she was going and then she could arrange a way to see him again.

"What about Martha? What about David?" Micah asked.

Benedict looked at him. "Did you follow us to come with us or to bring us back?"

"Shh, what was that?" Tommie looked into the darkness. "Someone's coming," she whispered. Benedict pulled out his flashlight and quickly scanned the shrubbery around them.

"Probably a critter." He clicked it off, afraid someone at the house might see, even at that distance. He looked back at Micah.

"Running away just seems a little extreme." Micah shrugged. "Besides, what about the others?"

"Yeah, what about the *others?*"

Benedict, Tommie, and Micah jumped as Sebastian and Eva appeared through the darkness.

"What are *you* doing here?" Tommie asked.

"Are you kidding me?" Sebastian responded in anger. They were both still wearing their pajamas under their coats.

"What are *you* guys doing?" Eva wrapped her arms around herself.

"We know what you're doing, and it's dumb," Sebastian said.

"Dumb for someone who's about to turn eighteen, so it doesn't matter. But what about you, Eva? You're not afraid of where they'll send you?" Tommie asked.

"They're working on keeping us all together," Eva said. "We just have to have faith."

Tommie groaned and hung her head back. She too was getting sick of those words.

"Where's Benny?" Micah jumped up and looked around him frantically. "Where's Benny, where's Benny?" They all searched the darkness, but Benedict had disappeared.

"Well, that's just great." Sebastian threw his hands up, exasperated.

"We have to find him." Micah's voice was trembling.

"I don't even know which way he went." Tommie looked around her.

"He'd have to go into the woods there. Any other way, he'd be headed back home." They walked in the direction of the tall dark trees, calling out to Benedict. When they reached the trees, the darkness intensified, swallowing them whole.

"Did anyone bring a flashlight?" Sebastian asked.

"Benny has the flashlight," Tommie said.

"I have one on my penknife." Micah searched his jacket pocket and a tiny stream of light appeared. "I suppose it's better than nothing."

"If we stick together, we'll be fine," Sebastian reassured them. "Let's chain up. I'll go first. Micah, give me the flashlight. Eva, you hold onto me, Micah hold onto Eva, Tommie hold onto Micah."

Tommie was not thrilled at being at the back, but she assumed Sebastian's plan was to put the strongest of the group at the front and back, so she was pleased all the same.

"Benny," Sebastian called. The others followed suit.

"Ouch, don't step on the back of my heels."

"Well, move *faster.*"

"Benny!"

"I can't see. I don't want to trip."

"Benny!"

"Ow . . ."

"You okay, Micah?"

"Yeah. Nearly twisted my ankle."

"You guys be careful, it's really bumpy."

"Last thing we need is to have to carry one of you."

"Benny!"

"You know where you're going, Sabe?"

"Let's hope so."

"Great, that sounds encouraging."

"If we keep going in one direction, we're bound to reach the other end."

"Here's hoping."

"Benny!"

"Ow . . ."

"What now?"

"I just hit a branch. Everyone be careful."

For a while they trudged and crunched and snapped their way without talking. They could only see as far as the flashlight reached. Beyond that was complete darkness. It was a darkness such as none the children had experienced before Sunshine Ranch, and each of them wondered if the others were just as scared as they were.

After what felt like twenty minutes, Tommie decided that she didn't like being at the back, no matter what Sebastian's reasoning was. She was holding in a fear that someone would reach out and grab her from behind. Taking deep breaths, she tried to think of something else. She thought about the times she had run away from her mother and new step-father. It had been all she could do to rebel against a situation that had been forced on her.

It had seemed obvious to her that her mother had made a choice between her daughter and this new man, and Tommie had lost. What hurt the most was the fact that it had seemed such an easy choice for her to make. She and her mother had been the best of friends, until the moment she met the man. Then everything changed, and a couple of months later, she had a new father. Although she never referred to him as such.

Then things changed again, this time for her mother. He didn't have to be a nice guy all the time, now that they were married. Her mother realized this, but not until her new husband had hit her for at least the fifth time.

Tommie had never been the victim of any of his violent outbursts, although her step-father always included her in his apologies by buying her a gift of some kind, along with a bunch of red roses for his wife. Until that point, his behavior had been concealed from the outside world, but he couldn't hide it the night he sent his wife to the hospital with a broken leg. Both Tommie's mother and her step-father concocted a story about how she had fallen while making her way down the stairs in the dark. Her mother had been dangerously in denial, and Tommie couldn't watch any longer, so she left.

Sebastian's voice broke into her thoughts. "Oh, no."

"What?" they all asked in unison, and then watched as Micah's flashlight flickered and died.

14

"WELL, THAT'S JUST *great*," Sebastian said, trying to see through the darkness, but it was as if someone had draped a black cloth over his head.

He reached out in front of him and felt nothing. The others couldn't even see the person in front of them, so they gripped each other's clothes for fear of being separated and lost in the abyss.

"Oh, Lord, please help us," Eva prayed aloud.

Sebastian suddenly had visions of news alerts reporting the disappearance of five children, with David and Martha standing behind a podium crying. What if they were found still standing in this one spot, but frozen to death?

"What now?" Tommie sounded nervous.

"Okay, you guys, just don't let go of the person in front of you," Micah said.

"I don't like this," Eva said. "It's creepy."

"*Benny*, if you can hear us, we *really* need your flashlight," Sebastian called out. They waited. An owl hooted nearby.

"What was that?" Tommie whispered.

"What?" the others asked at the same time.

"That . . . squeaking," Tommie said slowly.

"Nothing," Eva said quickly.

They hadn't moved since the light died. Sebastian took a small cautious step forward and then another and another. The others shuffled behind him.

"I totally hear something, you guys." Tommie's voice was shaking.

"Benny, come on!" Sebastian yelled out. He was angry now. Then they all heard the squeaking sound, and then the flapping.

"Okay, I gotta tell you. If that's what I *think* it is, I am going to scream."

"Please don't scream, Tommie, it's not what you think," Sebastian spoke steadily, but he was not convinced himself that the sound they heard was not that of bats.

"I'm telling you, if anything touches my hair, I will scream. I will *scream.*"

"Don't scream," a familiar voice said, and a light suddenly appeared a little way ahead of them. It moved quickly, searching the trees until it found them and shone on their faces. They covered their eyes until Benedict lowered the light to their feet. He was sitting on a large root under a tree.

"Benny!" Micah went to run to him, but it went dark again.

"Don't come here," Benedict warned. "I will keep the flashlight on, but only if you stay where you are."

"Don't be ridiculous, Benedict," Tommie said.

"I'm serious."

"Fine," Sebastian said. "So what? We have to stand here like this until the sun comes up?"

"No, you can have the light." He turned it on again.

"Benny, please. Let's just talk."

"I don't want to talk anymore."

"It'll be okay," Micah said.

"You think that it's going to be okay because you don't know what it's really like. You haven't been sent from one messed up house to another. You haven't been hit, or spat at, or punched for taking an extra cracker at lunch. No, you've had grandpa who fished with you, and a mother who sang to you every night. You had it good, so no wonder you have so much faith."

"Yes, I had all that, and now they are all gone, and who knows, I'll probably be gone too," Micah said.

"Well, I don't get why you have so much *faith* then. What good has it done you?"

"It's taught me never to give up, no matter how bad things get, because God has a plan for me."

"But your family's *gone*," Benedict insisted. "Your amazing family is gone."

"Yes, but God blessed me with them in the first place, if it was only for a short time."

"Yes, but then He took them away, and then He made you sick, and now you could die," Benedict said with gritted teeth.

"I don't know why He does the things He does, Benny. But I know He has a purpose, and I trust Him."

"But what about *us*?" Benedict blurted out. Micah was silent.

"You grew on us," Sebastian said softly. The more Benedict spoke, the more Sebastian understood why the boy was so angry. A foster child doesn't have much to start with, but to then lose whatever good comes along is just too painful a loss.

"You guys are like my second family. You *are* my family," Micah said. "Don't give up on me yet, Benny."

"Listen, you guys," Eva said, after a brief silence. "I don't know about you, but I'm really cold. We need to get back."

They all waited for Benedict to determine their next move. Finally, he sighed heavily, stood up, and shrugged.

"Fine." He walked toward them, handing Sebastian the flashlight.

***

The truth was that Benedict really *wasn't* sure that running away was the answer to his fear. As he had sat in the darkness listening to his foster brothers and sisters calling out to him, he realized that he'd found people who actually cared about him. *And what if Martha and David did find a way to keep them together?* he wondered. It was unlikely, but it wasn't impossible, and he'd miss out on that. And so, even though he wasn't sure whether his decision to return to Sunshine Ranch was based on his fear of missing out or a sudden faith that it would all work out, he didn't care right then. All he wanted was to go back.

Sebastian waved the flashlight around him, into the trees. "We need to go back this way." He signaled to a direction behind them with the light. They all grabbed each other again and treaded slowly back toward the ranch.

***

AFTER WHAT SEEMED like too long of a time period, Tommie asked, "Sabe, are you sure we're headed in the right direction?"

"We have to be, this is the way we came."

"This is the way we *think* we came," Eva said. "Don't forget, part of this journey was in pitch darkness."

"It *is* taking longer than it took to get to where we were," Sebastian agreed.

"Wherever *that* was," Micah mumbled.

Suddenly a sound in the distance chilled their bones and

they all stopped and listened.

"Uh . . . what was that?" Tommie's voice shook.

"Coyotes," Sebastian whispered.

"Maybe wolves," Benedict said.

The howls were heard again, overlapping and in short bursts before ringing out in chorus.

"We're going to get eaten alive," Tommie said in a harsh whisper.

"Oh, Lord, help us, *please*," Eva was pleading. "What're we going to do?"

"Okay, we need to stay calm or they'll smell our fear and come hunt us down," Micah whispered.

"Don't say that," Tommie said.

"I don't know which way to go." The sound of fear in Sebastian's voice worried everyone.

If he's afraid, who do we have to keep us sane? Tommie thought, but she dared not voice her thought, in case it strengthened the aroma of fear among the group. She took deep breaths, but it didn't help.

"How do we know we're not going in circles?" Eva asked.

"Don't *say that*," Tommie whispered.

"Oh, Lord, help us."

"We're *not* going in circles," Sebastian said.

"How do you know?" Tommie asked.

"I don't remember seeing *that* before." He pointed in front of them with the light, revealing a small, run-down shack. The sound of howls rang out again, and Tommie was sure they were getting closer.

"We need to get inside," Eva said hurriedly.

"In *there*? Are you *nuts*?" Tommie whispered. The dark cabin was hidden in trees. She imagined a crazy killer hiding inside, peeking out of the small grimy windows, chuckling to himself—maybe even muttering, "Yes, little children, come on inside." She shook the thought away.

"We have no choice," Sebastian said, taking charge again.

"Yeah, we do," Benedict said. "Get killed by some psycho hermit in the woods or be torn apart by a pack of wolves."

"This is *your* fault, Benedict," Eva spat the words out.

"*You cut that out, Eva,*" Sebastian warned. "Come on, we're picking the psycho." He moved toward the house, with the others rustling and tripping behind him.

The tiny porch at the front of the shack creaked under every footstep. Eva was whispering Hail Marys as Sebastian turned the handle and opened the door slowly. The howls rang out again, and this time it sounded as if they were being surrounded. The sounds still came from a distance, but they were too close for Tommie.

"Oh, please, get inside before we *die*," she begged. "At least we have a chance against the psycho hermit." She pushed them all inside and shut the door behind her. Once they were inside, they all held their breath, waiting to be jumped on or accosted. But nothing happened.

Sebastian scanned the small room with his light and they all watched as it revealed a surprisingly comfortable dwelling. The beam passed over a couch and a weathered leather chair beside a large fireplace; a modest pile of cut wood beside an old brass stand that held a shovel, brush, and poker; old, leather-bound books on an unfinished shelf; trinkets on shelves that lined the tops of the walls; and an unmade bed in the far corner. To the right was a tiny kitchen with a washed plate, fork, and cup drying on the counter and an old brass kettle on an ancient woodstove. The place was still lived in, it seemed, but there was no electricity. At least no one could find a switch or lamp anywhere.

"Let's hope that whoever lives here is on vacation somewhere far away," Tommie whispered.

"I don't know." Benedict touched the embers in the fireplace. "This is a fresh fire. I think it was lit sometime yesterday or maybe even this morning."

"What're we going to do?" Eva asked softly.

"We have no choice but to stay here tonight. It's too cold out there, and even if we survive the weather, I doubt we'll survive being eaten by coyotes."

Tommie joined Micah, who was sitting on the floor against the couch. The others followed, huddling together to keep warm. Sebastian sat between Eva and Tommie, who both leaned against his shoulders while the younger boys sat on each end, pushing in as close as they could get.

"You should probably switch that off to save the battery," Benedict said.

The light went out and they sat in complete darkness.

Sebastian hoped that David wouldn't be disappointed in him for not preventing this whole thing from happening.

Eva thought of Martha and prayed that she would not be pacing the kitchen, worried sick.

Tommie wished she was warm in bed, for this was the first time she secretly regretted running away from home.

Micah thought of his grandpa and the last time they'd stayed at his cabin.

Benedict wondered if he would be blamed for this.

"Eva?" Sebastian whispered.

"What?"

"You know what," Tommie interrupted.

After a pause, Eva began to pray: "Lord, protect us." Her voice encircled them in the darkness of the room. "Keep us safe from harm—"

"And please keep Martha and David from worrying about us," Tommie added.

"We're sorry, Lord, for not believing that You'll make it all right, in Your own way and in Your own time," Sebastian said.

"We will trust in You, Lord. Please forgive us for doubting You. Just please keep us safe, Lord, we ask this in Jesus' name," Eva concluded.

"Amen," they all said in unison.

Suddenly, at that moment, the front door flew open and Tommie let out a bloodcurdling scream.

15

TOMMIE'S SCREAM SCARED everyone more than the sudden entrance of the psycho hermit, and so everyone else screamed as well. Someone had kicked the flashlight in the panic and Sebastian groped for it in vain. The psycho hermit, with his own light, flashed it into each of their faces before speaking.

"Oh, for goodness sake, what are you all doing here?"

They all screamed again, but this time they jumped up and ran toward the voice they recognized, hugging the body they now knew belonged to Mr. Jones.

"Mr. Jones, thank you, God," Tommie said with an unsteady laugh. Mr. Jones also laughed, but his was awkward and filled with confusion.

He knelt by the fireplace stuffing kindling under the grate. Sebastian rushed to his side and helped scrunch pieces of newspaper into balls. The room was dimly lit by three lanterns that hung in corners of the room. Mr. Jones rubbed his nose with the back of his hand and glanced at Benedict who was standing by the couch with a furrowed brow and pursed lips.

"So what's the story here, then?"

Tommie volunteered to tell it, and began by recounting the truth about how she and Benedict were running away, and then how the others tried to convince them to go back. She sat on the worn out leather lounge chair as she told the story, ending with how they had become lost and scared and cold. Micah added that they had been surrounded by howling coyotes. Benedict shook his head and muttered that they were wolves.

"Basically, we could have *died*," Eva said in conclusion. She was in the kitchen, filling the kettle from a large flask of water.

Mr. Jones shook his head and piled three logs on the grate. Then he struck a match and lit the kindling. They all watched the flame catch and spread through the burning paper. Slowly the flames grew, stretching and dancing between the pieces of wood. It wasn't long before a full fire crackled and snapped, transforming the chilly cabin into a warm space, flushed by a golden, flickering glow.

Eva walked around the couch and sat next to Micah, who was lying curled on his side with his head resting on its arm. She reached out and touched his leg affectionately and he returned the gesture with a smile. Tommie sat staring absently into the quivering flames.

"Well," Mr. Jones said, arranging cups on the kitchen counter. "Let's hope we can get you all back before David gets up, so you don't worry anyone."

Benedict began walking around the room, glancing at objects that filled the shelves. Books had been lined up a long time ago, and trinkets strategically placed, it seemed, but they were now coated with a layer of dust. Eva cleared her throat and Benedict turned to see her look of warning. But he just shrugged his shoulders and gave her a "What?" expression.

He turned back to the shelf and reached out for a green

ceramic bowl filled with marbles. He smiled at the sound of discreet throat clearing behind him. The tips of his fingers wiped patches of dust off the surface of the small glass spheres. He grabbed some, letting them clink in his hand, and then looked at them. Among the marbles rolling in his palm was a dusty silver ring with three diamonds side by side; the center one much larger than the other two.

Benedict had never touched diamonds before and wondered if they were even real. And if they were, why wouldn't a poor man like Mr. Jones sell the ring? He glanced around him. *He sure could use the money. Maybe he's forgotten he has it.*

Mr. Jones began handing out cups of warm cocoa and Benedict returned the marbles. He held onto the ring a little longer, rubbing the dull stones with his thumb, but the shine was lost beneath the stain of time. He placed the ring back on the shelf, only this time next to the bowl of marbles, in a place where Mr. Jones would surely find it.

His eyes then fixed on the corner of a photograph peeking out from between two leather-bound books. He pulled it out and stared at the image of a beautiful woman with long brown hair, carrying two newborn babies. One was wrapped in a pink blanket, the other in blue.

"Who are these people, Mr. Jones?" Benedict carried the picture to the old man.

Mr. Jones smiled and whispered, "Ah." He took a moment to look at the image and then he sat between Micah and Eva. "These . . . are my wife and babies."

"Who?"

Both Micah and Eva leaned in on either side of him, and Tommie and Sebastian rushed to get a glimpse.

Benedict just stood and watched as Mr. Jones' sad eyes studied the image more.

"My family," he said softly.

"Where are they?" Tommie asked cautiously and Benedict was afraid to hear the answer.

"With God." Mr. Jones looked at them with a sad smile.

"I'm sorry," Micah said softly.

"Don't be," Mr. Jones said. "Almost thirty-seven years ago it happened, on a plane to Florida. She was on her way to visit her folks, to introduce them to their first grandbabies. I couldn't go. I was working for my father." He stopped as if regretting that decision for the trillionth time, and then he shook the thought away. "Anyway, they hit bad weather and . . . well . . . the rest is obvious."

They were silent.

***

Eva suddenly felt regret that they had almost taken Mr. Jones for granted. He'd been at Sunshine Ranch since before she had arrived there, but none of them had known his story. The only thing Eva knew was the brief tale David had told a year or so ago when she had asked why Mr. Jones ate dinner with them before going home every night.

David had explained that Mr. Jones had shown up in town when he, David, was just a boy. He began helping families out with odd jobs. Years later, when David and Martha opened their group foster home, they hired him to help around the ranch. For the most part, he accepted little in payment, even though he was poor. But it wasn't long before he became less and less like a handy man, and more and more like a family member.

Recognizing his quiet nature and his desire for privacy, no one had ever asked questions about his past. No one even knew where he lived—at least none of the children did, until now. Eva suspected now, after listening to his heartbreaking story, that he had left his home all those years ago to get away from the pain of losing his family.

Yet, you would never suspect it of him, since he had a smile for them every day and always a positive word to share. And so, without really thinking about it, she wrapped her arms around his neck and kissed his cheek.

"How do you guys do it?" Benedict asked, and they all turned to look at him.

"You just *do*," Mr. Jones said. "You have no choice, really, but to just do it. You take what God gives you, and you make the best of it. Only you have control of your happiness."

***

TOMMIE THOUGHT OF those words later as she sat in the darkening room after everyone had fallen asleep. The fire had reduced to red glowing chunks over hot sparkling embers. She couldn't relax. She looked around Mr. Jones' small, run-down home.

"You okay?" Sebastian's voice was a whisper, but it startled her in the darkness. He was on the lounge chair, looking at her.

"I was just thinking. This place is like a shack, but it's kinda cozy. It feels *safe*."

Sebastian leaned his head against the chair and listened quietly.

"Sunshine Ranch is a house, a barn, and land, but it's a home because of us who live and love inside it. And if we all had to leave, it really wouldn't be the end of us, would it? Not if we all stay together."

"But what if we *can't* stay together?" Sebastian asked.

She didn't have the answer to that question. She didn't even want to think about that awful possibility, so she didn't say anything.

"What's up with you and Faden?" Sebastian asked, as if the question had been on his mind for a while.

She smiled in the darkness as Faden's face came to her mind. "Why?"

"He's been talking about you a lot recently and I saw you guys take a ride earlier."

"Nothing, really. I like him . . . I guess."

"Yeah, that's what he said about you."

"Really?" Her smile blossomed into a grin. "Well, you don't have to worry."

"I'm not worried. He's a good Catholic boy. I was just wondering about you."

"Thanks a *lot*. I'm only fourteen, y'know."

"I didn't mean it like *that*."

"I know, I'm just kidding. I'd like to think I'm a good Catholic girl."

"As good as Eva wants you to be?"

"Better. Just don't tell her I said that." She heard him chuckle. "Sabe?"

"Hmm?"

"Thanks for being a good brother . . . type . . . person."

***

Mr. Jones woke them all early, while it was still somewhat dark. They trudged back through the trees, stepping over the rocks and roots that had tripped them up the night before. Micah trailed the group, and Benedict paused every now and then to wait for him. The journey out of the woods was not as long as their expedition in, but it was long enough for the sun to be rising and those at Sunshine Ranch to have awakened to the terrible reality of empty beds.

When Mr. Jones and the children entered the house through the kitchen door, Martha ran to them and hugged them each in turn before her expression changed from relief to anger. With her voice shaking, she demanded an explanation. David rubbed her back in an attempt to calm both her anxiety and fury. Nana Credence sat at the table with a red, puffy-eyed Isabella, who was watching the scene in silence.

Sebastian opened his mouth to speak, but didn't know what to say. He didn't want to say he had run away, because he, Eva, and Micah hadn't. At the same time, he didn't want to lay blame on Tommie and Benedict. His mouth was still open and Martha was still waiting for his response, when Tommie spoke up.

She made sure David and Martha knew that Sebastian, Eva, and Micah had not run away. Martha looked at her and Benedict, her own puffy, red eyes narrowed as she registered all the information.

Benedict nodded and listened and added, "We didn't want to be sent back to some awful place—"

"We don't know that that's going to happen, Benny," Martha said tiredly.

"Benny, Martha and I are working on avoiding that," David said softly.

"Yes, but what if you can't fix that?" He needed to make them understand that his intentions had been good, even if his actions were not. He needed them to know that he wasn't just "being Benedict," as Eva liked to say. It was the right thing to do, and he had to convince them of that or they would want him gone, just like all the other foster parents.

"Benny, nothing justifies you running away." Martha wiped her red nose with a crumpled tissue. "Do you think they'll let you come back if you run away? They'll think you *hate* it here and never let you back." She tried to remain calm.

"Running away will make it worse for you, Benny, you

have to understand that," David said.

"I didn't think we had a choice." He spoke firmly, but he knew his argument was weakening.

"That's *enough*." Martha was irate now. "You *have* a choice, Benedict." Her voice had become shrill. "You can run from the unknown and possibly miss out on being with us forever, or they can remove you kicking and screaming. At least with the second choice, you can take what you have now and be *happy* and *grateful*, and pray to your Lord and Savior that it won't change." Her face was red, and her voice trembled. She tried to take a steady breath. "Don't run away from where you're happy, just because you're afraid you might lose it. It's not over yet, Benny."

In the midst of the high tempered exchange, a groan was heard, along with the sound of a chair hitting tile. When they all turned, they saw Micah, unconscious on the floor.

16

MARTHA AND DAVID rushed to Micah's aid. "Get them out of here," David yelled to no one in particular, indicating the children who were crowding around them. Nana Credence and Mr. Jones directed them all out of the room, shushing their attempts to question what had happened and escorting them quickly to the great room.

"You children, please stay here until we get you," Nana Credence insisted. "Sabe, please?" Sebastian nodded and she closed the door behind her as she left.

Isabella started crying. Eva pulled her to her lap while the others sat quietly, trying to listen to sounds on the other side of the door. A while later they heard a car drive up to the house, all rushed to the window, but it was difficult to see who it was because of the trees that obstructed their view. About ten minutes later, other vehicles were heard crunching down the driveway. Tommie insisted she saw flashing lights, but Benedict told her to shut up. Sebastian told them all to shut up while he sat staring at the closed door.

After another agonizing hour, they heard the slamming

of car doors outside and the sound of departing vehicles. Then on the other side of the door came a dull wailing sound. It began as a groan and became a desperate cry.

"What's going on?" Tommie shouted at them, as if they had the answer, but they stared back at her in mutual distress. Isabella jumped off Eva's lap and ran to the door. Sebastian grabbed her before she opened it, and at that moment David walked in. His eyes were bloodshot.

Micah had died that day at Sunshine Ranch. While David broke the news to the children, Martha opened her arms to Isabella, who ran into them screaming. Nana clung to a bleary-eyed Tobiah, who had been sleeping, while Eva and Tommie hugged each other, crying. Sebastian held a confused Melanie close to him. Benedict ran out of the room.

No one could get Benedict down from the treehouse. The rest of the children watched from the window and the open kitchen door, as the sky darkened and storm clouds rolled in. It was the first storm since the one that caused so much damage to Sunshine Ranch. The same storm David had driven in to bring Micah home.

After watching the treehouse for a while, David, who had been sitting quietly over a cold cup of coffee, stood up and went outside. It was a strange sight to see the large man climb up the rope ladder of the treehouse as the rain began to fall. He crouched in front of the doorway for a few minutes and then disappeared inside.

The others waited in silence, glancing out the open kitchen door every now and then, eyes on the treehouse deck.

"Maybe I should go help." Sebastian looked at Martha for approval.

"Wait." Tommie was sitting on the counter looking out of the window. She pointed, and they all watched as David appeared with Benedict clinging to him like a tiny child. He carried him down the ladder, through the downpour, and into the house.

Later that evening, the family sat together in the great room. The sound of the crackling fire filled the space, and Isabella stared at the flames as she lay with her head on Eva's lap. She wondered if Micah was okay, and she thought about him being reunited with his parents and grandpa and God. *Do they have parties in Heaven?* she wondered. *Would it be a celebration with balloons and a cake and maybe even a banner that said, 'Welcome Home, Micah'?* She wanted to ask these questions, but thought they sounded really silly. Instead, she looked up at Eva and simply asked if Micah was alright.

Eva stroked her hair and said that Micah was in heaven, being taken care of by the angels. Isabella turned and looked at Martha for confirmation.

Martha smiled and said Eva was right. "God sees to it that everyone who has a good heart is loved." She pulled Melanie closer to her. The child was curled up asleep on her lap and Martha rubbed her cheek against the child's soft hair.

Isabella added angels to her visions of Micah's party.

"Benny," David said. "Would you like to come closer?"

The boy sat against the side of the sofa, legs outstretched, head down. He shook his head.

"Did you have something you wanted to ask about this?"

Benedict shook his head again.

"You know," David's voice was a whisper. "When I was a little boy, Nana always told me that the best way to mourn the loss of a loved one is to remember the good times." He looked at his mother, who rocked the twins in her arms. "You guys wanna try that?" He waited as the children tried to focus on memories of Micah.

Eva smiled as she recalled Micah's desire to build the treehouse and his desperate negotiations with each of the other children.

Sebastian thought of Micah's positive attitude, no matter what the situation happened to be, he always seemed to find the bright side.

"I remember when Micah fell out of the boat that time. That was funny," Tommie said, but the memory didn't cheer her up.

"I remember when he put a frog in Benny's bed and it peed on his pillow." Isabella chuckled.

"I remember when I went into Eva and Tommie's room and accidentally broke Eva's music box." Benedict looked up at Eva. The corners of his lips were turned down and his red, swollen eyes glistened. "I did it, Eva. I broke your music box, but Micah took the blame because he didn't want me to get in trouble." He covered his eyes with his arm and moaned, unable to control himself. "Why did he do that?"

"Oh, Benny, come here." David reached out for him, and this time the boy went to him.

"I was so mean to him. Why did he do that?"

Benedict squeezed into the space David and Sebastian made for him. David hugged the boy tight with both arms and kissed his head, looking over at Martha with a pained expression.

"Because he loved you," Martha said.

Benedict didn't understand. When he insisted that he was always mean to Micah, David said that he wasn't really being mean. Martha nodded in agreement and added that they were just being brothers, and that's what brothers do, but that just didn't help Benedict. He still felt an awful pain in his stomach. He wished so desperately that he had been kinder to Micah, and he hated the fact that he couldn't go back in time and make it up to him.

***

THE DARKNESS FILLED Benedict's room, closing the walls in around him. He tried to remember what life was like before Micah, but all he could recall was his own selfish dismay when he found out that a new boy was arriving at Sunshine Ranch. Now the guilt soaked through him and he couldn't sleep, because Micah's face was engraved in his mind. And then there was that ache, wedged inside his chest. Now that Micah was gone, it felt bigger and it hurt more. He wished he could take a deep breath and blow it out of his mouth.

"Are you there?" The sound of his own voice surprised him, and he felt silly talking into the darkness. He waited, not sure for what. "I've never had a home like this one before. I guess you already know that." He sighed loudly. "If you're there, and there's something you can do, please help." He turned to look at Micah's bed and wished he was there. "I'm sorry," he said more softly. "I should've been better. I should've given you a chance." Benedict hugged his face with his arms. "I was scared," he whispered. "I'm scared now."

He lay like that, with visions of Micah and the rest of the Credence family consuming his thoughts.

***

NOBODY SAID A WORD the next morning, as the Credence family ate their breakfast around the table. They were all dressed in black. Mr. Jones got up and grabbed the coffee pot and filled Nana's cup.

Tommie walked into the room, also dressed in black, but

that was her usual color. What was different, however, was her usual attempt to hide—her face was clean of black makeup, her nose ring was missing, and she had even washed out the color in her hair.

Although the rest of the family was taken aback by her transformation, they still didn't say anything. It was an understanding that didn't need clarification in words. Tommie kissed Martha, who held her close for a few seconds before touching the girl's face, looking deep into her eyes, and kissing her forehead.

"Hi," Martha whispered.

"Hi," Tommie responded.

That's when Martha got to meet the real Tommie.

The doorbell rang and David left the room. When he returned, Faden, his parents, and Roy were behind him.

"We're so sorry."

Faden's mother held Martha. Faden's father spoke quietly with David and Mr. Jones, and Faden hugged his friends. When he reached Tommie, he took a moment to look at her face. He didn't smile or say anything, he just held her a few moments longer than the others, and then he placed a soft kiss on her hair.

All the while, Roy stood in the background, raising his head now and then to watch the solemn exchanges, his own expression sullen.

***

A LITTLE MORE than a week before Christmas, the snow fell fast and thick as Martha looked out the kitchen window, watching as the sparkling flakes appeared from the blackness of the night sky. On the ground, it glistened like a jewel covered blanket, concealing the imperfections. Martha wished that it would stay that way forever—untouched. She had wanted her family and her life to stay untouched, as well, but they were being trampled and intruded upon, just as the glistening quilt would be tomorrow.

She recalled how somber Thanksgiving had been. The children had tried so hard to be happy, but she knew they all missed Micah, as if he had left them the day before, instead of almost four months earlier. Martha knew that they appreciated their blessings, but they missed Micah, and so did she. He had been with them for only three months, but he'd touched each of their lives in such a way that a lifetime would not be enough to forget him. She closed her eyes tight, bit her lip, and took a deep breath.

She turned to see her family huddled around the kitchen table, where bowls of frosting and bags of assorted Christmas candy were spread in disarray around a large partially-built gingerbread house. Celine Dion was singing, "O Holy Night" in the background. Martha reached up to the advent wreath that hung over the dining table, and picked out the third plastic candle she had forgotten to turn on for that week. She scolded herself for not keeping at least her faith together during this distressing time. She snapped the switch and it flickered.

"Benny, stop sticking kisses everywhere. You're messing it all up," Isabella complained before taking a bite of her Twizzler.

"Hey, it's my personal creativity. Besides, this doesn't have to take forever, y'know." Benedict continued to stick Hershey Kisses in every vacant spot on the house.

Martha put the candle back. She recognized a difference in the mood of the room compared to past years, and she wished she hadn't agreed to the gingerbread house-making tradition. David had been the one to talk her into it, saying that he didn't want the children to think that *everything* was changing. She looked at David now. He was trying to make Tommie laugh by wedging two pretzel sticks into the top sides of his mouth, like walrus tusks. He was even wearing his extra-long Santa hat, also a custom for the occasion.

Martha could tell that Tommie was feigning her laugh, just as everyone else was forcing their enthusiasm. *Lord, how could I have ever thought that this would take their minds off our problems?*

What made it harder for Martha was knowing that her children wanted to be happy for her and David's sake and, just as at Thanksgiving, they were trying to make the best of their situation.

Benedict and Isabella continued to bicker and no one wanted to intervene.

Eva stood back to view their creation and Martha noticed her vacant stare.

"Hey, Eva, are you okay?" she asked.

The girl seemed to come out of her trance. "I feel empty. I feel like I'm not connected to anything, and I can't get out of it."

She didn't know what to say in response, because she felt the same way. In fact, they all shared that feeling.

Just then, the phone rang and Martha left the room.

It was Miss Davis. "Mrs. Credence, we just wanted to check in on the status of your situation."

Martha's heart sank. The only plan they really had at this point was to get through Christmas, and then, when the new year came around, to start looking for a new home. But that really wasn't a solid enough plan for Miss Davis, Martha knew, so she decided to be brief.

"We're doing well, Miss Davis."

"You have nothing to report?" Miss Davis was obviously pushing for more details.

"Well, in the case that we do have to move from Sunshine Ranch, I'd like to assure you that we will be able to bring all the children with us."

"Well, as you know, there are certain requirements expected of foster parents. And it's our understanding that you've pretty much over-extended yourself, as far as space."

"Yes, but we've managed to make it work very well here. The children are very comfortable, and I'm confident that we'll be able to make it work anywhere."

"I'm afraid that may be too vague of an assurance. It might make more sense to find your new location first, and then we can discuss which children can remain in your care."

"Which children? Miss Davis, I don't want to have to choose between my children, I want them all. Besides, after losing Micah—"

"Let's take it one step at a time, Mrs. Credence. There is another concern that would affect this whole situation."

"What would that be?"

"The mother of young Isabella Jameson has regained her right to custody."

"What does that mean?"

"She wants her back."

17

"WHAT DID YOU SAY?" Martha whispered the question.

"Isabella's mother wants her back, Mrs. Credence. We have scheduled a transfer date of December 22nd."

"But that's just a week from now." She covered her mouth with her hand. She felt a lump form in her throat.

"Well, her mother would like her child back for Christmas. Besides, there really is no need to prolong any upset."

She didn't hear the rest of what Miss Davis had to say. The ache in her heart had her full attention. She placed the receiver down just as David entered the room.

"What now?" He asked as soon as he saw the expression on her face.

"Bella," she said softly. "Bella's mother wants her back."

David sat down and said nothing.

"What is going on?" She looked at her husband, her expression distorted with anguish, tears forming in her eyes. He just shook his head. "What's going on? We lost Micah. We're going to lose this house. We're going to lose the children—"

"You have to hold it together," he said in a low voice.

"I'm trying, David, I really am, but it's getting harder every day."

"I know, but you can't lose it. The children need us. If we fall apart, who are they going to look to?"

"David, how am I going to tell Bella that she has to go back? She'll be devastated. It's the nightmare she has every night. It's come true."

***

ISABELLA'S NIGHTMARES centered upon one event. She remembered it clearly, because it was a reminder that her mother's words might come true one day.

Isabella had no father—her mother had told her so. "Some kids just have one parent," she had explained badly. "That's life, Isabella. That's just the way it is." She had been getting ready to go out and leave Isabella alone to cry in the dark until she fell asleep, as she did every night. On that particular night, a storm had raged outside her window. Lightning flashed and cracks of thunder shook her in her bed. She cried out louder than she had intended, and the sound was too much for some of the neighbors in the apartment building. Soon Isabella had heard voices outside the door of their one-room studio apartment. Some were familiar, but she was not sure. Then there were knocks at the door, and she hid under her blankets. Her mother had warned her never to answer the door, even if the person on the other side said he was a policeman. "They're probably lying."

As Isabella lay there, she sank deeper and deeper into the bed. Even when she heard her name being called, she stayed where she was. Finally, there was a huge bang and a bright burst of light filled the room as the door flew open and people charged in.

The group was headed by two policemen, followed by her neighbors.

"See," one woman said, pointing to Isabella, who was petrified in the bed. "See, there she is all alone again."

Mrs. Edwards from downstairs rushed over to Isabella's side and hugged her. "It's okay now, Isa. You're safe, little girl."

From that moment, everything became a blur for Isabella. She remembered being taken from the room that same night and sent to another woman's home, where she spent the night. She didn't see her mother again until one day in front of a judge. The neighbors had also been there, and they had all cried. But her mother never did. She shrugged and argued and shook her head a few times, until the judge banged his gavel and Isabella was allowed to say goodbye.

"I'll get you back," her mother had said. But it sounded more like a warning than a promise. Isabella was brought to Martha and David's that same night. She could still feel her mother's aggressive kiss on her cheek and sometimes, if she thought really hard, she could remember her face. But the words, she would never forget: "I'll get you back," her mother had said. "I'll get you back."

And these were the words that woke Isabella up in the middle of the night.

When David and Martha entered Isabella's room that evening, she knew she wasn't going to like what they had to say. It was apparent that they were trying to hide sadness with feigned smiles. It didn't work. At first she was afraid that something bad had happened to someone. Then, when David and Martha told her about her mother, she realized the something bad had happened to her. David was the one who broke the news to Isabella. He told her that it was actually a good thing that her mother wanted to make things work.

Isabella's first concern was for the babies—he didn't want to leave them. She covered her face while Martha rushed to her side and David knelt in front of her. He continued to focus on the positive, telling Isabella that the best place for a child is in the loving arms of the parent, but Isabella wasn't convinced. She tried hard not to cry, because her mother wanted her back. But then she thought about being alone in the dark and she began to sob.

"People change," Martha whispered. "And I'm sure they wouldn't let you go back there if she's not willing to change."

The next morning at breakfast David and Martha broke the news to the rest of the family. The children looked stunned, not just because Isabella was leaving, but because they only had a week left with her.

David put his hand up to stop any rush of questions. "Listen, this is the way it works. We've been lucky not to lose you guys, and now that the 'system'"—he signed quotation marks with his fingers—"is, in a sense, working, Isabella is lucky enough to be able to return home and be with her mother. We should all be happy for her."

But the children didn't look happy. Isabella didn't look happy.

**

BENEDICT SAT ON A rocking chair on the porch, wrapped in a blanket. Fat, puffy flakes dropped slowly through the still air. Nothing moved but the falling snow. He lifted his blanket higher over his frozen cheeks so that just his eyes peeked out. A chill rushed through him and he shuddered. Never had he expected that anyone would leave Sunshine Ranch, except for him. Now Micah was gone and

Isabella was on her way.

He didn't want to go inside. They were all still mourning the loss, even though she still had two more days before a car would come and take her away. He had been avoiding her, mostly because he didn't know what to say to her. They had argued a lot, and she got on his nerves most of the time, but he didn't want her to go.

As if reading his thoughts, Isabella opened the screen door and peered out. She saw him and disappeared back inside. At first he was grateful, but then hurt, because it seemed as if she didn't want anything to do with him either.

A few moments later, the screen squeaked again and she reappeared with a blanket wrapped around her and sat in the chair next to him. They were quiet for a long time, and he guessed that she, too, was just looking for a place to think. After a minute he looked over at her and she turned and looked at him. Then his hand found its way out from under the blanket and he laid it, palm up, on the arm of his chair. She looked at it and then at him and then she reached out and held it.

***

THEY ALL SAT AROUND the kitchen table, waiting for the car that would take Isabella away from them. Martha had pulled her onto her lap and was holding her close, breathing in her scent. She wanted to have it to remember always. She had already kept two unwashed t-shirts that she could inhale.

"I want to say that things happen for a reason, or that we need to have faith, or that God has a plan, but none of these things seem comforting at this moment."

"I know that, Martha." Isabella tried to smile. Her eyes were red and swollen. "It's okay; I'm one of the lucky ones, right? I get to go home."

Nana Credence blew her nose. "Well, this will always be your home too."

Martha was battling her emotions as she hugged the child. She had to hold it together, just as David kept saying, for Isabella's sake. But she was still afraid of what might happen to her little girl.

A car honked outside and they all looked at each other and then at Isabella.

***

THAT EVENING WHEN EVA walked into her room, she found Tommie organizing her comics on the floor. She'd never seen the carpet on Tommie's side of the room. But now her books were neatly lined in her bookshelf, and there were no clothes to be seen. Her closet doors were fully closed, and she had even folded her pajamas and hung them at the foot of her bed.

Tommie looked up surprised. When she saw Eva's stunned look, she narrowed her eyes and said warningly, "Don't even say anything." She placed the pile of comics on the bottom shelf and stood up.

Eva walked to her bed and lay down facing the ceiling. Tommie lay on her own bed. They both lay silent until Tommie said, "Hey Eva, aren't you forgetting something?"

Eva smiled and then reached for her music box.

***

It was Christmas Eve and the Credence family sat around the table eating a lunch of tomato soup and cheesy bread. Faden and Mr. Jones were among them. Martha reluctantly grabbed the mail from the counter before taking her place at the table. She looked around at each child, seeing the gaps where Micah and Isabella belonged. The only sound was the children eating, and her heart ached as she watched them. She understood that they each held a great burden within them that was shrouded in fear of the unknown, prompted by the fear of their pasts.

She sighed as she opened one bill after another. The money from the Credence Variety Show was gone and Nana's donation wouldn't last long. To make matters worse, David had had to put off the phone calls to prospective clients until after the Christmas season. Martha shuffled through the rest of the mail, deciding to leave the remaining bills for another day.

She looked up and saw David watching her from across the table. She smiled sadly at him, knowing that he was feeling their pain also. She opened a Christmas card from Miss Madden and then one from Faden's parents. When she picked up the next envelope, she knew it wasn't another bill, but it was too thick to be a Christmas card.

She didn't recognize the scratchy blue handwriting on the yellow envelope. Her heart jumped, and she was afraid to open it. She discreetly showed it to David, who shrugged his lack of knowledge. Finally, her curiosity exceeded her fears and she tore it open and unfolded the document inside. She waited a couple of seconds before she allowed herself to read.

She felt the color drain from her cheeks.

David must have seen, because he asked, "What is it?"

"A miracle," she whispered.

The children turned their attention to her.

He pushed his chair out and went to her, and she handed him the papers. The children waited as he read to himself, and then exchanged a look of complete bewilderment with Martha.

"What?" Tommie asked, mid-chew, finally breaking the silence.

"We're not sure." David folded the papers up quickly.

He looked at her and then quickly at his mother and Mr. Jones, who stared back, waiting. He mumbled something about a phone call and left the room.

Everyone turned to Martha now, who was looking into space. Eventually, she returned her attention to them and asked, "Who's for hot chocolate?"

Nothing was said about the papers in the yellow envelope for the rest of the day.

18

THE news spread fast. "They say it's a miracle," Miss Madden said to one of the female parishioners as she handed her a program for the Christmas Mass.

The other woman nodded knowingly. "The angel," she said.

"The angel?" Miss Madden asked, confused.

The woman nodded as if she'd been privy to undisclosed information. "That's what they're calling him. The angel."

"How do they know it's a 'him'?"

"Oh, they don't . . . just 'the angel.'"

Parishioners shuffled in past them, careful not to slip on the floors wet from snow people tracked in with them, despite the towels Mr. Jones had laid down to try to keep the floor dry.

Miss Madden continued to hand out programs while she and the other woman continued their conversation. Another woman had been listening nearby and approached them.

"Do you think maybe it was Mr. Green?"

"Merry Christmas, Mrs. Flanagan." Miss Madden

handed her a program.

Mrs. Flanagan ignored the greeting and threw herself directly into the discussion. "They say he's the only one who could pay such an amount." She stretched her neck and searched around, trying to find Mr. Green. The small church was filling up swiftly.

"Okay, ladies," Miss Madden said nervously. She didn't like the direction the conversation was going. "Let's take our seats now."

Fr. Thaddeus discouraged gossiping, and she didn't want him to find her in the midst of a huddle of whispering women.

"But—" Mrs. Flanagan began.

"No, we must move along and let the others in. Mind your step, the floor's a little wet." She gently nudged both ladies in the direction of the pews.

***

WHILE THEY WAITED for the Mass to begin, the parishioners looked around, trying to catch a smile or glint in an eye somewhere that would give away the secret—or perhaps the face of a stranger, someone who knew about the misfortune of Sunshine Ranch and wished to save it. Everyone was searching for clues that day, except Mr. Jones, who was 'resting his eyes,' and Mr. Green, who stared ahead without any expression at all.

"He looks mad," Benedict said with a satisfied smile.

"I'll say," Tommie added.

"Hush." Nana Credence placed her finger on her lips as the music began. They all stood. The procession commenced.

At the end of the service, before the final blessing and prayer, Fr. Thaddeus took his place behind the pulpit, adjusted his festive white chasuble, and beamed over the congregation.

"Before we conclude this Christmas Mass and go off to celebrate the birth of our Lord and Savior, Jesus Christ, I must make a confession," he began. "I have never been surprised at the workings of our Lord. He is an awesome God, a good God. He is an all-powerful God. Why should I be surprised by *any* miracle that takes place?" He paused, then went on, "Including the one that we've *all* been pondering today. And it happened during Christmas . . . of all times."

"There is no limit to God's greatness and I know this, and yet I am in awe of it, *every* day. I see it in the eyes of every infant. The way a child is formed in a mother's womb from a tiny egg into a living and breathing baby. I see it in nature's way of sustaining itself. In the way that there's no limit to love. I see it every day. And I see it today in the pure kindness of a mysterious person—a person who wishes to give, but asks for nothing in return, not even recognition. Not even a 'thank you.' A selfless, selfless act, and again I am in awe of it all."

He bowed his head. "Let us pray . . . God, we thank You for sending us an angel who has given a most generous gift. An angel who is so obviously full of love for the Credence family. An angel who sees how much this family has done for children in need of a loving home. We thank You, Lord, for the Credence family, and this blessing that allows David and Martha to continue in their endeavor to give children hope. And, God, we thank You again for Your miracle, Your angel, who has taken the spirit of this town and lifted it so high."

Fr. Thaddeus sniffed, and took a moment to regain his composure. "You have shown us yet again, Lord, that everything is possible. On this Christmas day, the day of Your Son's birth, You have shown us that there is still so much good in this world. Thank You, Lord. We praise You endlessly in Jesus' name, Amen."

He wiped each eye quickly before looking up and smiling. "Oh, it is a great day today. A great day, yes, for Jesus Christ was born this day and Sunshine Ranch has been saved. Bow your heads for God's blessing."

***

AS WONDERFUL AS the "angel's" gift was, Martha knew there was still one thing she needed to make her happiness complete. It was about a week after Christmas Day, when she couldn't wait another minute, she picked up the phone and dialed.

"This is Miss Davis."

"Yes, Miss Davis, this is Mrs. Credence at Sunshine Ranch." As she spoke, Martha stood looking out of the kitchen window at the children playing in the snow. She smiled as she watched all the kids attack her husband with snowballs, and a bittersweet feeling came over her.

"Oh, good day, Mrs. Credence, and may I also say congratulations on your windfall."

"Yes, it's definitely a blessing." She rolled her eyes, but told herself to be kind and patient. It was a new year after all, and they'd had a wonderful Christmas, thanks to the angel. And thanks to the angel, they would have so many more wonderful memories to share at Sunshine Ranch.

"I was hoping to get in touch with Bella's mother," she went on. "I have some Christmas gifts I'd like to forward to her."

"Bella?"

"Yes, Isabella Jameson."

"Isabella Jameson." The woman muttered the name. "Remind me again, please?"

"She's eight years old, blond hair, blue eyes—"

"Descriptions mean nothing, I'm afraid. We have so many blond-haired kids in foster care."

Martha held in her anger and recited Isabella's case number. She heard a tapping of keys while Miss Davis muttered to herself on the other end of the line. After asking Martha to repeat her question, Miss Davis finally said, "Well, let me see . . . it might make more sense for you to send the items here, so we can forward them when she's settled."

"Okay . . . wait, 'settled'? It's been nearly a month, did they move?"

"Yes, she just moved again."

"I don't understand. Where did her mother move to?"

"Well, Mrs. Credence, I really cannot give you information on this child, since she's no longer in your care."

Martha's heart started beating faster. She sensed something was wrong, just by the way Miss Davis had rushed through that last sentence.

"Miss Davis," she began to say in a low voice, trying to remain calm. She didn't want to upset the woman, but she had to get to the truth. "What *can* you tell me? Isabella has been my child for almost three years."

There was silence on the other end of the phone, then a loud sigh.

"Mrs. Credence." Miss Davis was especially careful in her wording. "This information comes off the record and I only tell you because I do believe that you care for these children."

"Okay?"

"Miss Jameson has lost custody of Isabella again. She left the child alone for three days. I cannot tell you more than that."

"Can you tell me where she is?"

"She's been relocated."

Martha tried to hold in her excitement. Could this be another miracle? Would she get her Bella back? "Can't she come back here?"

"That's not possible."

"Why? We can stay here now. We're not going to lose the ranch."

"I understand that, but there was still a concern, prior to you losing the farm, that you had overextended yourself."

"Miss Davis, now that our finances are back in order, we'll be able to make some additions to our home. We're even thinking of including a formal classroom."

"I'm sorry, Mrs. Credence, but I really cannot discuss this with you further. Isabella has been relocated and it would be best not to disrupt her any more. I would suggest that you forward the items in question to me, and I will see to it that she gets them."

The line went dead. That was it. What was she supposed to do now? She knew one thing, and that was that there was no way her Isabella would be pushed off to some other family who had no idea who she was or what she needed, especially when she already had a family at Sunshine Ranch.

Martha stood with the phone still in her hand, her mind racing. She took a deep breath, rushed to the kitchen door and flung it open.

"David!"

***

THE CHRISTMAS SEASON was coming to a close and, even though the snow was still falling regularly, there was much work to be done in repairs inside the house and barn. And they now had the funding to do it right.

David re-hired Faden on a more regular basis. To Tommie's utter embarrassment, he and Martha sat both her and Faden down to inform them that they and Faden's parents would be keeping an eye on them, now that they had an emotional interest in each other.

"Not that we don't trust you," Martha added quickly.

"We trust you," David reiterated. "Just don't give us any cause not to." They nodded and stood up. "Oh, and Faden, Tommie will not be dating until she's seventeen." Tommie covered her face. "Oh, and there will be no more kissing." Tommie groaned with embarrassment.

"Not a problem, sir." Faden nodded. "My parents feel the same way." He looked over at Tommie with a smile. "We can wait."

Faden was then dismissed, and both Martha and David proceeded to mortify Tommie further by reiterating God's desire that she remain pure until marriage. They'd had this discussion with her before and, just as before, Tommie nodded without speaking, feeling her face burn up. When they were satisfied that they'd covered everything, Tommie left the room quickly, declining Martha's offer to answer any questions she might have.

The phone rang and David went to answer it, while Martha joined Faden, Tommie, and the others in the kitchen. About ten minutes later, David walked in, his face pale.

"What?" Martha asked wearily.

"Nothing, we just have a lot of repairs to do before the John Miller team arrives this spring."

"What?"

"Yeah, something about three horses biting riding school kids, another one throwing a rider, and how my services are the best," he said, singing the last three words with a grin.

***

A WEEK OR SO LATER, the children sat swaddled in coats and blankets on the porch, just as the day was ending, watching the sun set behind the frozen trees. Faden was showing Tommie and Eva how to play his guitar. The sky glowed, and splashes of crimson and orange colored the heavens.

Tommie watched the car slush down the drive toward them. "David's home."

As the car neared, she added, "Who's that with him?"

They all stared, trying to get a glimpse of the person sitting in the passenger's seat.

Sebastian leaned forward to get a good look.

"Are you serious?" he exclaimed, grinning. He jumped up and ran through the snow to the car, whooping with joy.

"What?" Tommie looked into the car. "Are you kidding me?" She got up and followed Sebastian.

Eva was still confused, but she, Faden, and Benedict rushed after them.

Martha appeared at the door with Nana and the little ones. She was grinning about the secret she'd been keeping. Now, finally, they could all share in her joy.

"It's Bella!" Tommie shouted.

"*Bella!*" they all yelled. Melanie and Francine jumped up and down in the doorway screaming, "*Bella Bella,*" while Martha laughed.

David opened the car door, releasing Isabella into the chaotic mass that swarmed around her. Martha walked toward the group, waiting for her turn to hold the child. Isabella eventually appeared from within the group and ran to her. Martha held her close and tight.

"Mama Bella, I missed you so much."

"This is amazing!" Tommie yelled.

"Well, let me just explain that Bella is here to *visit,*" David told them.

He was bombarded with a mix of, "What?" "Awww," and "Why?"

"It's okay," Bella said. "My new foster family is really cool, and they said I can visit whenever I want."

"How'd you do it?" Eva asked David excitedly.

"We didn't do it."

"Who?" Sebastian asked.

It was then that Sebastian learned that his father had played an important role in allowing Isabella to visit Sunshine Ranch. He had been an influential man before his time in prison and, since being released, he had worked hard to earn his reputation back. He knew people in the legal world who were willing to help Isabella get visitation with the Credence family.

Isabella laughed and gave Benedict a hug. "Did you miss me, Benny?"

He shrugged, trying hard not to show his own happiness. "Maybe a little," he said reluctantly. "I had no one to pick on."

A few weeks after Isabella's visit, Martha and David called the family into the great room. Nana Credence and Mr. Jones were sitting on the couch next to the fireplace. The adults all wore serious expressions.

"What now?" Sebastian asked Eva in a low voice, but she merely shrugged in response.

"We have some news," Martha said.

"Martha and I have come to a decision," David said. "This year has been a really difficult one for all of us. What with losing Micah, then the possibility of losing the house, then the possibility of losing all of you, then actually losing Bella, well. . . ." He paused as if for effect and then said, "Well, we can't go through that again."

"Fostering children is a difficult thing." Martha rubbed her hands together nervously. "The emotional rollercoaster is just agonizing, and I don't know if I can do it anymore."

"Martha, what are you saying?" Eva tried to keep her voice steady.

"Wait!" David put his hand out. "Hear us out." He was stern in a way that the children had never seen before.

Martha said, "We've done our best as foster parents. We've loved you, and cared for you as if you were our own. But the truth is, you're not our own."

Someone gasped, and the children stood stunned, staring at the people who had saved their lives.

Eva felt a hand slip into hers and looked to see a wide eyed Francine. She squeezed her hand, herself feeling angry and betrayed. *How could they be saying this?* She wondered.

It can't be true, Tommie thought.

It's all over, Benedict concluded.

Sebastian picked up Melanie and held her close to him.

David glanced at each of the children. "Well, I think we should just come out with it, Martha."

"Fine." She shrugged. "You tell them."

"Fine." He cleared his throat and announced, "Martha and I have decided that we don't want to foster you children anymore."

19

SUDDENLY AN OUTBURST of cries and yells filled the room.

"How could you?"

"You don't want us?"

"Why?"

"QUIET!!!!" David yelled in such a thunderous manner that all the children stopped and stared back in terror. *"We don't want to foster you children anymore . . ."* He looked at each child in turn, then said with a smile, "We want to adopt you."

The room was silent. The children were speechless.

"Well?" Martha's pursed lips were now grinning. She searched each child's face for a clue about how they felt, but she didn't have to wait long for their response—they all rushed her and David, jumping up and down, hugging each other and the babies, while David and Martha laughed.

"Are you guys kidding?" Tommie bounced gleefully, then ran to hug Nana Credence and Mr. Jones.

David put on an absurdly serious expression. "Do I look like I'm kidding?"

Melanie pointed and giggled. "You have a funny face."

"No, *you* have a funny face." He took the little girl from

Sebastian's arms and held her tight. "And *soon* you will be *my* little funny face."

Benedict had not moved, but stood still among the lively crowd.

"Benny, come here," Martha said. She smiled and walked slowly over to him, then held her arms out to him. "Oh, little Ben, can I be your mom?"

"You can't just *adopt* us," Benny said, but then asked cautiously, "Can you?"

David nodded. "There are details we have to take care of, but we wouldn't say something like this if we hadn't already taken care of the obstacles . . . that's all I'm going to say. But the ball is in your court. It has to be your final say."

Martha's eyes were still on Benedict when she repeated her question to him. Slowly he nodded, and then his pursed lips formed a tiny smile, right before he ran into her open arms.

***

"SEBASTIAN, JUST BECAUSE you've turned eighteen doesn't mean you have to leave." Martha stood with her arms crossed, watching her oldest boy pack a suitcase.

"I know, Martha." He laughed. "And you know I'm not leaving."

"Well, it feels that way," she responded. "What if you like it in France, and you don't want to come back?"

"Are you kidding?" He looked at her. "I couldn't love any place that much." He walked over to her and hugged her. "Martha, it's only a month."

She picked up a shirt that lay on his bed and folded it slowly. "Trust your father to pick a graduation present that keeps you all to himself."

Sebastian laughed. "Well, he can't keep me away from

you. I'll be back before you can miss me."

"I already miss you." She hugged the shirt.

David walked into the room. "Martha, are you harassing him again?"

"Yes, but it's not working. He's still leaving us."

"Poor, Martha." He wrapped his arms around her waist. "You know, Sabe, you'll have to send us a postcard every other day. Martha will want to know everything."

"Trust me, I know. I've already been given the run down."

"Are you going to do this to every child that leaves us?" David asked her with a chuckle.

"Every one."

***

TWENTY-ONE YEARS LATER, a cell phone rang on a bedside table in an uptown New York apartment. It hadn't woken Benedict up, because he had barely gone to sleep. He reached out in the darkness and grabbed for it. *'Sunshine'* flashed in front of him. He watched for a moment, waiting for her to go into voicemail.

"Little Ben," he heard her say in his mind. "It's Martha. I was just thinking about you and wondering when you could take some time and visit. I know you're busy, but we miss you. Please call. We love you."

He rubbed his face and looked out of the window. It was snowing again. Snow in the city was nothing like snow at Sunshine Ranch. Here it wasn't crisp and white and clean and pretty. It wasn't the sparkling snow from Narnia. New York City dirtied the snow and mutilated it in a way that offended him. It was slushy and brown and a pain in the neck to travel in.

He picked up the phone. Martha hadn't left a message this time, and he was surprised and a little disappointed.

The time was 4:36. *Maybe a quick workout before the office will get me motivated.*

"BENEDICT? BENEDICT!" Jack Benson was an associate at the newspaper where Benedict worked. He wore his usual brown plaid jacket over a crumpled white shirt. Benedict didn't care much for the man, but it had become his own private amusement to aggravate him. The two men were submersed in the chaos of a busy newsroom.

Benedict continued to stare at his screen full of words, trying to focus his attention on his story, but that was getting more difficult as his enthusiasm for the news slowly dissipated.

"Listen, some of the guys are getting together at Sparky's tonight, thought you'd like to join us." Benson leaned against Benedict's desk.

"I wish I could." Benedict pretended he was engrossed in his article, but didn't hold back on the sarcasm that had become his standard personality trait.

"Okay, so what do you have going on tonight? Another dinner party? Drinks with an old friend? Secret girlfriend? What?"

"I have a meeting with my parole officer." Benedict's eyes never left the screen.

"Fine, forget it. Spend your nights alone, moping about who knows what. I won't be bothering you again with an invite."

"Thank you."

"Jerk."

Benedict scolded himself for his rudeness. He closed his eyes and sighed. Then, looking back at his screen, he realized that he couldn't think. He literally couldn't keep a thought in his mind. He couldn't read the words on the screen, and even if he could, they didn't make any sense to him.

"Forget it," he whispered, shutting off his computer. Grabbing his phone, he walked out of the chaos in search of his mind.

He crossed the busy road and dodged a splash of slush thrown up by a cab, his head filled with the sounds of car engines, angry horns, and people yelling on cell phones. He gritted his teeth, pulled the collar of his coat higher around his neck, and quickened his pace. There was nothing to look forward to in his journey, so he would make a detour. That was all he had these days, and he needed it.

Ahead of him, he saw a woman walking with a little girl about three years old. The child kept stopping to stomp on snow banks. The child's mother was visibly frustrated. After yanking the girl's arm several times, the woman finally grabbed her forcefully by the jacket, literally lifting her off her feet, before dropping her next to her. She smacked her on the bottom and legs, then grabbed her by the hand and pulled the now-crying girl along with her. As he passed the two, he heard the woman say, "You better quit crying or I'll give you something to cry about when we get home."

Benedict's heart suddenly began beating at a furious rate and he turned to face the woman, not sure what he intended to do or say.

"Wow," he said loudly. His body was shaking.

The woman looked up at him, her eyes wide with fear, and she pulled the girl close to her.

He laughed. "It's amazing how you can get her to listen to you by just beating her. What a unique concept." He started to walk away, but then turned. "You don't need to protect her from *me*, lady. I need to protect her from *you*."

Benedict shook his head, shocked at his own behavior. But he knew the difference between a swat and a smack, and he shivered at the thought of what happened to that little girl behind closed doors.

He turned up the next road on the right and kept going past a line of brownstone apartments. When he saw the large white steps ahead of him, he quickened his pace. At the top of the steps, he opened the large wooden doors into the church and left the world outside. He tapped his finger into the holy water and signed the cross, inhaling the scent of incense into his lungs and allowing the feeling of holiness to envelope him. He walked to a pew, just as a priest not much older than himself walked up the center aisle. He wore a long black robe and had a short, neat beard and a receding hairline.

"I see it's that time again," the priest joked.

"Excuse me?"

"I see you here at this time almost every day. Although I've never seen you here at Sunday Mass."

Benedict frowned. "Is that okay?"

"Of course it is. I was just making an observation." The priest smiled. Benedict was about to sit when the priest said, "Are you here for confession?"

"Uh, well, I was just hoping to sit for a while."

"Of course, take all the time you need . . . and of course if you would like to talk. . . ."

"Talk about what?"

"Whatever." He shrugged. "You look like a man who needs to talk."

"I do?"

The priest nodded. "I've seen many a pained expression." When Benedict said nothing, he added, "I'm sorry. My intention is not to pry, but to offer you some solace."

"I know," Benedict said. "I guess I wouldn't even know what to talk about. I'm feeling a little. . . ." He gestured with his hands, but he couldn't find the right words. He couldn't find any words.

"Agitated?" the priest suggested.

Benedict looked at him and responded, "Yes . . . unbelievably."

"Please sit." The priest held his hand out.

Benedict took a seat and the priest sat next to him.

They were quiet for a few seconds until the priest said, "My name is Father Richard, by the way."

"It's nice to meet you. I'm Benedict." They shook hands.

"Actually, I have a confession of my own."

"Excuse me?" Benedict was confused.

"I know who you are, Benny. We've met many times before, a long time ago." The priest waited and Benedict searched his features, his smile, and his eyes, and although he saw something, he could not put his finger on it. "Let me just say one thing." His voice was shaky as he added, "I'm sorry for calling you a reject."

Benedict's mouth opened, and he saw suddenly that it was the smile that reminded him that this man was Faden's brother, Roy. The boy who had been so unkind to them all those years back. He tried to remember the last time he'd seen Roy, but he couldn't remember much after the short visit when Micah died. Roy had left them alone.

"Richard?" Benedict asked.

"I got a new start." He smiled. "Just like you."

Benedict looked the priest up and down and then pointed to his garb. "What happened to you?"

"There's often a defining moment in a person's life that changes them forever." Fr. Richard raised his chin, his eyes glazed over. "That moment for me occurred in your kitchen, the day my family came over to offer our condolences for losing Micah."

"Why?"

"I was a conflicted child, Benny." He shook his head. "I wasn't pleased that my brother seemed more like a brother to all of you than to me. I didn't understand why he picked foster children, who had been left by their own parents, over me. I was his own blood after all. So I tried to demean all of you so he would see, but it backfired. He continued to love you all more and me less." He raised his eyebrows and waited for a response.

"Well, he loved *one* of us more than the rest." Benedict chuckled.

"Yeah." Fr. Richard smiled awkwardly and Benedict could see that there was more. "I even prayed that something bad would happen to all of you, and then Micah died."

"You didn't do that."

"I know that now, but back then, when I saw you all in pain for a boy you'd known just months, I thought I was the most awful person. All I wanted was to belong."

"I'm sorry."

"No, don't be sorry. The moment I left your home, I swore that I'd devote my life to doing good. I chose this and I'm happier now than I've ever been."

"Well, then, it's me that envies you now," Benedict muttered and looked down at his hands. His fingers intertwined.

At that moment his cell phone buzzed in his pocket and he reached for it. He saw *'Sunshine'* before turning it off. A wave of guilt washed over him and when he looked up, Father Richard was watching him.

"I'm lost," Benedict said softly.

The priest nodded and pressed his lips together, but he didn't say anything.

Benedict gazed ahead at the large crucifix elevated over the granite altar.

"I'm living a life, but I don't feel alive," he muttered. "I get up in the morning, go to work, fulfill my duties, get paid, go home . . . and for what?" He turned and looked at the priest again. "When I was a child, I looked forward to this point in my life, so I could finally be in control, but . . ." His voice cracked. "I'm not in control and I feel that if I don't find a sense of relief soon, I'm going to explode."

The priest nodded again. "You know, you can only really belong to something when you fully give yourself to it."

Benedict mulled the words in his mind for a moment. He was about to ask what he meant when Fr. Richard added, "You can only give yourself fully when you let go of your fears of letting go."

You can only give yourself fully when you let go of your fears of letting go? Benedict was so confused now, he didn't even know what question to ask, so he decided just to stay quiet.

"You're not alone, Benedict, trust me," Father Richard said. "God is ready to help you, to strengthen you. You just need to let Him in."

Benedict looked back at him blankly. He had prayed at times, but maybe that wasn't enough.

"When were you last home, Benny?"

"A really long time ago," Benedict muttered. "But I have a trip coming up for work. Maybe after that . . ."

He had hoped that after talking to Father Richard, he'd feel some relief, but now he was feeling more anxious than ever. They sat in silence for a moment.

"Don't be discouraged, Benny," the priest eventually said in a low voice. "You're here, after all. Just remember though, He will only help those who ask."

In the silence that followed, Benedict smiled. "You know, I hated going to church when I was a child."

"Yes, I did too. It seems we have a lot in common."

"But I come here every day because it brings me peace, and because it's the only place that takes me home."

"It sounds to me, Benny, like you'll find what you really

want when you go back home," Fr. Richard said. "My only question for you is . . ." He pointed to Benedict's chest. "Why are you so afraid to go?"

20

THE man in the red pickup opened his eyes and immediately noticed that the day had eaten a few more hours. He had fallen asleep. He rubbed his face and started the engine. He took one last look at the scene and headed down the meandering dirt road toward it.

The place was too quiet. Even though the late summer day offered its usual symphony of birds and crickets, it was all silence to him. He reached in his pocket and felt the warm key between his fingers. This would all be real again in just a few moments. The fourteen years between now and the last time he was here would suddenly shrink into almost nothing, and it would feel as if he'd never left.

A flapping sound caught his attention and he smiled before he looked up. The flag was still flying, just as he'd predicted, but it wore the scars of many years.

He stepped onto the porch where the once-white rockers still sat and planters hung in sad disarray. The door unlocked easily and when he walked into the house, he gasped. It was smaller inside than he remembered, but this house held so much in it.

Benedict stood for a moment, taking in the combined

smell of polished wood and mold. A mouse scurried across the wooden floor and under a skirt of white cloth that covered a piece of furniture. Everything was covered in cloth soiled with seven months of time. Even the pictures on the walls. He didn't touch anything as he walked slowly through the room. He glanced up the stairway, hesitated, and decided not to go looking up there just yet. This was all too much already.

Instead, he walked through the living room into the kitchen, his steps echoing throughout the house. The fridge was stripped of the memories that once smothered it. A vase with dead flowers sat in the middle of the oversized wooden dining table. This had not been covered. He reached for the vase and carried it out the kitchen door to the overgrown back yard.

He walked through the overgrown grass to see the one thing he wanted to see more than anything else. The tree stood in front of him, doing its best to stand tall. Its strong limbs still hugged the wooden house, as if protecting it from harm. He placed the vase on the ground and walked closer, as if hypnotized.

When he reached the base of the tree, he looked up into its leaves and reached for the ladder. He tugged it to be sure it was still sturdy, then climbed up, squeaking with every step. The treehouse was surprisingly spacious inside. The walls were bare but for a few drawings of flowers, and one of a horse. He knew them to be Peachie and Melanie's artwork. The lantern hung from the ceiling, and the little bookshelf still housed a few old books and comics. He dusted off the dirt and dead bugs and fumbled through them, shaking his head as he came upon his old favorites.

Then he stopped and noticed a familiar green and yellow striped book sticking out of the back of the bookshelf, as if it had fallen back there years ago and been forgotten. He stared at it before reaching for it, and then he stared longer as he held it in his hand. Afraid to open it, he wedged it into his back pocket.

When he turned to the open doorway, he envisioned David peering in all those years ago, and his eyes stung. He took a deep breath and exited into the bright sunlight again, where he lay back on the little deck and looked up into the leaves. Strings of Christmas lights were still draped around the limbs of the tree. He felt the pain that had lodged in his chest so many years ago—long before he could even remember—slowly begin to dissolve. For the first time since he had left this place years ago, he felt as if he was finally home.

***

THE FAMILIAR TASTE of sugary goodness filled his mouth and triggered many more forgotten recollections. He smiled happily, knowing he must look goofy to all the other customers in Milly's Cafe, but not caring one whit. He wanted to laugh, and cry, and sing, and shout aloud, all at the same time. Why had it taken him so long to return to this wonderful place?

As he looked around, he recognized a few faces, older now, matured with time and experience. He wanted to tread carefully. He wanted to take his time. He wanted to work his way back on his own terms. It was bad enough that this lemon meringue pie was pulling him through a hall of memories while he pressed his heels to the ground in a failed attempt at slowing down the pace. Some things he had no control over.

His phone began to vibrate in his pocket and he pulled it out. '*Work*' flashed in front of him. He stared at it for a few seconds and sent the call to voicemail, and then savored another bite and looked around him again.

Benedict's eyes stopped on a young woman who was looking right back at him from the corner of the room. Alone at a table with her own half-eaten piece of pie, she leaned back and stared at him with narrowed eyes. She did not smile, but after a moment, she got up, grabbed her plate, and walked over to where he sat.

"Little Ben?" Her eyes were still slit in an almost accusing manner. But she seemed to know, and sat down opposite him anyway.

Now that she was so close, he could see the deep blue eyes—they were unmistakable. His heart rapped against his chest.

"Bella." He spoke softly, looking into her eyes.

She nodded and smiled and they stood up to hug.

"I knew it. I knew it the moment I saw you." They sat again. "But it was the expression you made when you took your first bite of Miss Milly's pie . . . well *that* was the real giveaway."

"Bella," he whispered again and shook his head slowly.

"Yes, it's me." She laughed at his look of total bewilderment. Then her face became serious. "I was wondering when you would come."

He shrugged. "I've been crazy busy."

She nodded, but her eyes told him that she didn't really believe him.

"At least you came, I suppose." She took a bite of pie.

"I just needed it, I guess. Work has been consuming a lot of my time, y'know. I can't seem to get away from it." He smiled as he watched her scrape her plate clean. "I just needed time away and I couldn't think of anywhere better than here."

"Too bad about Sunshine closing, huh?"

"Yeah, what is going on with that? I tried calling. Where are Martha and David staying?"

Benedict recognized a look of confusion in Isabella's face, but when she bit her lip, his stomach lurched. "What?" He was afraid to hear her response.

"Benedict, I. . . ." She seemed to change her mind about how to break her news. "Benny, David died."

"What?" It was a gasp for breath more than it was a word. His chest tightened and he gasped again.

"Are you okay?"

He nodded his response, but he couldn't look into her eyes.

"He died seven months ago." Isabella spoke gently, reaching out for his hand. "Martha couldn't deal with it . . . she still can't. She's staying at the Taylor Home right now. We were afraid of her living alone. She stopped eating; she stopped taking care of herself; it was awful. And she refused to let any of us take care of her."

"Why didn't anyone tell me?"

"We *tried*." She leaned toward him.

Benedict wanted to be angry, but deep down he knew that he had made himself unavailable to them, traveling for work and changing apartments. He'd never been able to settle down. It was his fault. He thought about all the times he put Sunshine into voicemail. It was his fault, and now it was too late.

"We tried to find you, but you never answer your cell, you obviously don't check your voicemail, and you're always off somewhere covering a story when we call your office."

Seeing that she was angry, he wondered if his behavior had instilled this emotion in all his brothers and sisters, or worse, Martha. He stood up abruptly, startling her, and threw money on the table. "I'm sorry." He stumbled his way out into the sunshine where he took a breath.

Isabella followed him out. "You should see her, Benny.

It's like she can't seem to function without David. Oh, Benny." His forehead furrowed with anguish, and she reached out to him.

He looked around aimlessly and then marched toward his truck. "I have to go and see Martha."

"I can come with you, if you like."

"No," he said, without turning around.

He wanted to go alone, because he didn't want Isabella to see him fall apart. He didn't want her to see him pull the truck over and wail out loud into his steering wheel. He didn't want her to see him ask God why He took David before he could tell him that he loved him for making him whole again; for changing his world in a way he never thought was possible.

The Taylor Home was a large colonial-style assisted living facility on the other side of the lake. Styled like a fashionable inn, it had a large porch and vibrant gardens. Benedict entered the home cautiously, afraid to see Martha there, but not sure why.

Music was playing in the entranceway. Some residents sat on couches alone, and others sat in groups, but hardly anyone spoke. He was stopped by an aide, who first asked for identification and then led him down a hallway. The residents didn't acknowledge him. The aide seemed kind enough, and the place seemed nice enough, but it still wasn't where he wanted to see Martha.

They continued on down the hall, passing bedrooms, until they reached what looked like a game room. Some of the residents sat at tables, playing cards or checkers, while others crocheted, or knitted, or read a book. One resident sat alone in a rocking chair, looking out of the window but seeing nothing.

Benedict took a deep breath. He watched Martha for a moment, trying to compose himself before approaching her with a feigned smile.

She recognized him immediately and stood up, reaching both arms out to him. She was still beautiful and much stronger-looking than he had imagined. But she definitely looked older than her age, and thinner. The shine in her eyes was gone.

"Little Ben." She laughed softly while her eyes filled with tears. "I had a feeling this morning that I would see you soon. Oh, my boy."

Benedict had promised to be strong for her, but it became difficult the moment her arms surrounded him and he inhaled her scent—a mix of Dove soap and cocoa butter. He bit his lip. He felt like he was ten years old again, and the magic of her hugs brought his past rushing back to him.

"I'm sorry I wasn't here," he whispered into her neck. "I'm so sorry."

He hadn't meant to get upset. She, after all, had lost the love of her life. Suddenly, a rush of thoughts entered his mind. How could he expect her to comfort him? Where was he all those years when they all needed him? Hiding in some faraway country, pretending to be a journalist.

"Oh, stop." She held him at arm's length. "You stop that right now. You know David would not have you hurting like this."

"I just wish I . . . I wish I. . . ."

"Hush." She stroked his hair and held his face so he couldn't avoid looking into her eyes. "He already knew . . . he already knew . . . okay?"

"Okay," he whispered, but it still wasn't okay to him.

He spent the rest of the day with Martha, holding her hand and telling her about his life back in New York, his news adventures, and his travels. She *oohed* and *aahed* and told him how proud she was of him, and how she knew that all her children would do amazing things.

Benedict didn't think anything he did was as amazing as what David and Martha had done for him and the others. When the time came to leave, he kissed her cheek and stood up, and he told her he would visit her the next day.

"When do you have to go back?" She still held on to his hand, as if afraid to let it go.

"I don't know." And he really didn't.

His heart raced as he drove back to Sunshine Ranch. He was afraid it would burst out of his chest. He needed to be there sooner than the car could take him, so all he could do was take deep breaths out of his open window. *Lord, help me,* he prayed. *Lord, calm me, please.*

Once there, he staggered to the back of the house and threw himself into an old, worn-out deck chair. He looked out to the field, up beyond the farm and into the woods where he and Tommie had tried to escape that night, so many years ago. He stared for a long while, listening to a wood pigeon cooing in a tree. Then he remembered Micah's photo album and pulled it from his pocket. He stared at the cover, working up the courage to open it.

The first picture was of Sunshine Ranch at its best. The sun was setting and the children sat on the porch smiling for the camera. The next picture was of David with Captain Jack. The next shot was of Micah taking a picture of himself—he was making a face. Benedict's eyes glistened, but he allowed a short, soft laugh to escape his lips. The next picture was of them all in the treehouse. Another showed them all holding up their catches after a fishing expedition. He recalled the actual moments some of the pictures had been taken, and knew that each occasion was as happy as the photo depicted.

He stopped flipping the pages and went back to the ones he'd already glanced at, staring at his own face in each shot.

His chest hurt and he tried to calm his breathing by sucking in deep breaths. He shut the book and put it back in his pocket.

He gazed at the field, where the overgrown grass was waving to him. Pushing himself up into a sitting position, then onto his feet, he began to walk, not knowing where he was going. He felt his phone buzzing in his pocket, over and over. *Oh, God, help me, please.* He wondered if he was having a heart attack. It wasn't unheard of. His mind wandered to an old colleague at his office who had had a heart attack at the age of twenty-four. Stress had been a major factor. *I've been stressed all my life.*

He entered the barn and leaned over a stall door, inhaling the stench of horses that had become glorious to him. Closing his eyes, he thought about how he would give anything to go back to early mornings mucking out the stables with David. *David.* He thought about his first morning, when David invited him to muck out with Mr. Jones. *You can only give yourself fully when you let go of your fears of letting go.*

He opened his eyes. The words had come to him from nowhere. His mind then drifted to Nana, then Eva, from one person to another and then another and another. Dizzied, he felt as if he was going to pass out, so he trudged back to the house.

The sun was still hot, wearing him down, but the breeze was intoxicating and he used it to pull him onward like a soldier crossing the desert. While he couldn't remember a time when he was free of worry, he had never experienced this level of anxiety, and it scared him. He stopped and gazed up at the blue sky, begging for relief. He closed his eyes and waited, feeling warm tears fall from the sides of his lids.

"I hear you."

He felt a wave rush through him and opened his eyes. He had heard the voice as if it was whispered in his ear by someone standing next to him, but he was clearly alone. Was it his own voice? But he knew that wasn't true. He made his way back to the same chair and reclined there motionless for what seemed like hours, the voice resonating in his mind.

"I hear you. I hear you."

It was the bright lights of a car descending the curved driveway that eventually awakened Benedict from his trance, and to the realization that the sun had set on him.

21

BENEDICT WATCHED the car descend the driveway and then disappear on the other side of the house. He groaned at the thought of having to interact with anyone, but was relieved to see Isabella walking toward him, hugging a brown bag of groceries.

"I brought dinner and invited myself," she called to him.

"Thank you." He meant it more than she realized.

Forty-five minutes later, they were sitting at the table in the back yard, dining on grilled steak tips, asparagus, and garlic potato salad. He took a sip of his red wine and looked up at the treehouse, now illuminated with hanging camp lamps for lack of electricity.

Isabella followed his gaze and smiled. "Takes you back, doesn't it?"

"More than you realize."

"Is that a good thing?"

"What do you mean?"

"Well." She cleared her mouth. "From what I can remember, you never seemed happy here."

"Really?" But he wasn't surprised by her comment.

"I remember . . . you seemed so angry all the time."

He shook his head. "I was such an idiot. I haven't changed much."

"Don't say that, Benny. We love you, no matter what."

"Oh, gee, thanks." He looked at her with mock appreciation. She bit her lip and he sighed. "See? Still an idiot." He took another sip of wine.

"Anyway, that's not the point. Well it is partly, but . . . I wasn't angry." He laughed to himself and shook his head, looking up at the treehouse. "I was actually the happiest I've ever been."

"You were?" She raised her brow in surprise.

"I know." He sipped his wine and leaned back in his chair. "I wasn't angry, I was happy. But more than that, I was vehemently afraid."

His phone vibrated in his pocket and he reached for it. *Work* flashed across its display.

Isabella stood to take their plates into the kitchen, offering him a private moment to answer. Reluctantly, he did.

"HQ wants you for a piece in Hong Kong next week, can you do it?" Benson sounded agitated, and Benedict knew that if he didn't take the assignment, Benson would have to. His colleague hated international flights.

"I can't. I still have a few things to tie up here."

He cut the call short after that. The call had shattered the moment and reminded him that the fleeting serenity he had felt was not real. Sooner or later, he would have to go back to New York and continue his mediocre existence.

He sat staring into the darkness. The moon and stars shone so bright—he'd forgotten that they actually existed. He could hear Isabella in the kitchen, scraping plates. She only had a lantern to guide her way, until the power company turned the electricity back on the next morning.

He didn't know how long he would be here, but right now, he didn't want to even think about leaving.

"You know what I think?" Isabella called from behind him. "I think we should have a little party. Get everyone together—a reunion—now that we have you here. That in itself is cause for celebration."

Benedict smiled. He could feel her standing at the open door, waiting.

"Sure, why not." To himself, he added, "The prodigal son returns."

"Great. Of course we'll have to fix up this place." She disappeared back into the kitchen.

***

BENEDICT WOKE up at 4:02 a.m. the next morning, his mind too stirred up to go back to sleep. He'd had a dream, it seemed, but it felt more as if God had whispered His plan. It was so obvious to him now that he wondered why it had taken him so long to figure out. He stirred restlessly, turning from his one side to the other, checking his phone every minute, although it felt like ten. But he couldn't contain his anticipation and sat up with a groan. Raindrops tapped on the window.

He grabbed his blanket and went downstairs to sit on the porch and watch as a monsoon came to fruition. The experience was breathtaking. He gazed out through the rain to where the fog rose up and smothered the mountains in the distance. He wanted to cry out with joy, and tell the world that he had a plan and he would be home soon.

It was true that his present way of life kept him busy, and his job paid well, but it lacked emotional fulfillment. Why should he plod along when his empty existence was leading him in the direction of a breakdown? There had to be a better way. He closed his eyes and listened to the rain douse the world around him. It was wiping his slate clean.

Just then, a familiar car drove in through the streams of rain and Isabella came running out, carrying two cups of coffee. She screamed as she ran through the shower onto the porch and Benedict laughed.

"Nice." She handed him his saturated cup. After setting hers down, she wiped her face with her hands, and pulled her soaking hair back from her face. "What're you doing up so early?" She settled next to him with a sigh.

"I couldn't sleep. You?" He popped the lid off his coffee and blew into the cup.

"I wanted a cup of coffee, and I figured you could do with one also."

"Thanks." They both sat back to watch the scene. *This feels good*, Benedict thought. *Almost perfect.* He looked at Isabella and she gazed at him. He lay his hand on the arm of the chair, palm up, and Isabella took it, smiling.

"I've missed you, Benny."

"Yeah, well, can't really blame you."

***

MR. GREEN had aged pretty well. His face was a little thinner, and his hair had all turned white, but he was still the distinguished man he had been years ago.

"Well, Benedict—"

"Benny."

"Of course." He laughed and extended his hand. "Benny, it certainly is good to see you here."

"It is?" He shook his hand, never imagining that Mr. Green would be so cheerful to see him. As a boy, he'd never made an effort to be polite. In fact, he'd resented Mr. Green for a long time, simply because the man had money.

He scolded himself now for being so contemptuous of a

person he didn't really know. It seemed so ridiculous and unfair. *Isn't that the same as hating someone because he has great parents?*

A growing realization that he'd been wrong about a lot of things was making him feel worse and worse about himself by the minute.

"You know, all you Credence children were very special to the townspeople."

"Really?"

"Absolutely. So what can I do for you?" Mr. Green gestured toward a chair and took his own seat.

"I want to buy Sunshine Ranch." He had not known that this was his plan until this moment, sitting in front of Mr. Green. He had only planned to see what his options were to stay in the area, but as soon as he said it out loud, it seemed to be the perfect solution.

"Okay?" Mr. Green looked confused.

"Yes, that's . . . that's what I'm here for. To buy the house from you."

"From me?"

"Well, the bank, of course, not you directly."

"The bank?"

"Yes, so . . . uh . . . how do I go about making that happen?"

He could not purchase the ranch outright, but he had saved enough to offer a good down payment. He couldn't imagine why the bank would refuse.

"Well, Benedict—I mean, Benny—the bank doesn't own the ranch."

"Really? You mean Martha still owns it?"

"No, the person who bought it years ago . . ." The banker turned to a filing cabinet, and began to search through it.

"If I recall, it's in trust," he muttered, half to himself.

"Yes, here it is." He extracted a folder and reviewed the paperwork inside, nodding slowly. "Yes, that's right, just as I remembered it."

22

BENEDICT was confused. "In trust? So who owns it?"

"Benjamin Jones." Mr. Green tilted his head back a little and narrowed his eyes as he looked down through his glasses at the paper in front of him. "You may not remember him."

"Bones?" His forehead creased down low over his eyes.

"No, *Jones,*" Mr. Green repeated slowly.

"Yes, yes . . . I know who you mean. Of course, I remember him. But he died."

Mr. Jones had passed a few months before Benedict turned eighteen and left the ranch. It had been a very sad occasion. It seemed as if the whole town had attended the funeral.

"Are you telling me that *Mr. Jones* owns the farm? How is that even *possible*? He didn't have a penny to his name."

"Oh?" Mr. Green chuckled. "Yes, it did seem that way, didn't it? But, no."

"What do you mean?"

"What I mean is that Mr. Bones, I mean Jones, was a very wealthy man, but refrained from defining himself as such."

"I'm *so* confused." Benedict shook his head, as if shaking off a ridiculous thought. Then he remembered the night he and Tommie had run away—he'd found that diamond ring in a bowl of dusty marbles and wondered why a poor man had been so careless with such a treasure.

"I can imagine your confusion, but the fact is, he bought the ranch."

"So *he* owns it."

"Well, since he passed, it's been in trust."

"What does that mean? In trust for whom? For Martha?"

"No."

Benedict felt as if his mind was spinning. "Then forgive me, Mr. Green, but who owns Sunshine Ranch?"

"Well . . ." He looked at the paperwork again, then at Benedict. "Tell me something, Benny. Why do you wish to buy the ranch?"

He cleared his throat. "I want to reopen it."

"Reopen it?"

He nodded. "I want to give abused and neglected children the same gift that was given to me and the other Credence children."

The other man smiled. "I'm glad you said that."

"Why?"

"Because now I can tell you who owns Sunshine Ranch."

"Who?"

"*You* do."

"Excuse me?"

"You. You see, the agreement that Mr. Jones drew up specifically instructed that the first Credence child to take interest in said property, for the continuation of a foster home . . . well, he or she would get the home."

Benedict was speechless.

"You see," Mr. Green continued, "according to *this*"—he tapped the paperwork—"And of course I'll have to go through this again with a fine-tooth comb, but if I remember correctly, Mr. Jones' wish was that Sunshine Ranch continue on as a home for unwanted children."

"Why was no one informed of this?"

"Well, Martha Credence is still the lawful resident until . . . well, you know. And when the time came . . . well, it would have been a waiting game really."

Benedict started to pace the room in disbelief. "Bones was the miracle," he said to himself.

The banker overheard the comment. "Mr. Jones said he would buy the home and be responsible for all its financial burdens."

"Did Martha and David know the truth?"

"No. Everything was arranged through me because the bank was in the process of reclaiming the home. It was a really awful time for your family. I'm not sure if you remember." Benedict did remember. "Anyway, David and Martha received a contract stating that Sunshine Ranch would remain in their control, but that it would be backed financially through another party."

"Why didn't he want anyone to know?"

"He didn't want that recognition. He lived a peaceful life and he didn't want that to change."

"Wow, and he had all that money the whole time?"

"He wanted for nothing but happiness. He found happiness in wanting nothing." Mr. Green looked down at his desk. "I learned a lot from that man," he said more to himself than to Benedict.

"Why give that money to *us*?"

"Why should it surprise you?" He looked at Benedict. "He loved Martha and David and all you children. He loved you all. You were his *family*. And it was *nothing* for him to give it all to you, just so you could stay in town. Just so you could stay together."

***

IT TOOK NEARLY a week to restore Sunshine Ranch to some semblance of its past life, although it still lacked so much. Right now it was just a house. Benedict hated the way his steps echoed throughout its structure, emphasizing its emptiness. He hadn't told Isabella about his plan yet. It was still all pretty surreal to him. He thought about how wonderful it was going to be, filled with children again.

Isabella helped him prepare all the bedrooms, and the memories in each room were overwhelming. It was as if he'd forgotten them all until the day he returned. *Why was I so eager to forget a life that gave me life?*

***

ISABELLA SCRUNCHED her face up in disgust and peered at the tiny stud in her fingers. "I think I found one of Tommie's old nose rings."

Benedict laughed. "Return it to her."

He flipped through an old comic book. They were organizing Eva and Tommie's old room. Isabella dropped the ring into the already full trash bag, then threw herself onto Eva's bed and glanced at Benedict.

She'd been intrigued by him from the moment she saw him at Milly's. She was thrilled that he'd returned to Sunshine Ranch, but still wondered why he'd come back after many years of avoiding them.

"So you were telling me about how you were afraid of being here as a child," she said carefully.

"I wasn't *afraid* of being here." He flipped a page. "I was just afraid that I'd be sent away."

She could see the little child in him as he read the comics and smiled to herself.

Finally, he looked up at her seriously. "I didn't want to be *forced* to leave this time." In response to her look of confusion he added, "I know. So many idiosyncrasies for such a small child, but it made sense to me. If I were to leave, it'd be on my *own* terms. Even though I'd come to settle down, I still had a deep fear that I'd be uprooted again, and for the first time I didn't *want* to leave. This time I'd found the home I *wanted* to be at. But the idea that I could stay was just not real. I was just not *that lucky*. And because I was so desperate not to get hurt again, I disguised my fear with . . . belligerence."

"Ooh, and I thought you were just a big fat meanie head."

He smiled. "I want to show you something."

He retrieved the photo album from his pocket and handed it to her.

She flipped through it. "Oh, wow, look at this. Oh, look at the babies, how cute were they, oh, and Franny . . . do you think we ever got a picture of her *without* her finger up her nose? Look, it's Micah and me, oh, wow. . . ."

"Look at *me*," Benedict said after a minute.

"I know, you were cute too." She rolled her eyes in a playful manner.

"*No*," he said sternly. "Look closer."

"What?" She recognized the seriousness in his tone.

"*Look at me*." He spoke through gritted teeth and pressed his finger onto an image of himself.

She flipped another page and he pointed to himself again.

"I just had this permanent frown *wedged* up there on my forehead." He gestured toward his brow. "Martha was right. I was so afraid that I was going to lose the happiness, that I was never really *happy. Look at me.*"

Isabella looked up at him without a word and saw that his eyes had become watery.

"What a *waste of a life*." He reached over and grabbed the book from her. "I have to see Martha." He got up and headed for the door.

"You want me to come?" She hoped that he would accept her invitation this time.

He turned to her, but his eyes looked to the floor. "No." He left the room.

***

BENEDICT NEEDED to tell Martha about his plans. He felt it would solidify his decision. He needed to hear what she had to say, but more than that, he had something to say to her. He decided to take her out to dinner. He couldn't stand seeing her in that place.

"Oh, Little Ben," Martha said when she heard his news. Her eyes seemed brighter than before. "If anyone can do it, it would be you."

He smiled at her genuine happiness. "I want you with me, Martha."

"Of course, I will always be with you."

"No, I mean, I want you to come back to Sunshine Ranch and stay there with me."

"Oh, Benny, I don't know if—"

"Please, Martha. You belong there and I need you. The children will need you."

"But they'll have *you* now."

"Martha, *please*," he said with more urgency now. He reached out for her hand. "You don't have to do anything, just be you, that's enough . . . that's *more* than enough." He squeezed her hand affectionately. "It was enough for all of us. *Please, Martha.* You have no idea how much that would mean to me."

The waiter came to their table and filled their water goblets, while Benedict tried to compose himself. When they were alone, he tried again.

"Martha, you and David changed our lives. There is *nothing* that we can *ever* do to repay you for that."

"Benny." She touched his face.

"*No.*" Becoming more adamant now, he shook his head. "I *need you to understand this.*" He swallowed hard. "You loved us so much . . . and we felt it *every day.* 'I love you' and 'thank you' are not strong enough sentiments to communicate our feelings for you and David . . . I just don't know. . . ." His words got stuck in his throat and he swallowed again.

"Benedict," she said softly. "Loving you children, that was the easy part."

"Martha," he whispered. She waited, her eyes narrowed as his expression became more pained. He tried to divert his eyes, but he needed to look at her when he said this.

"What is it, little Ben?"

"Martha, I just have to tell you that I'm sorry."

"What? Sorry for what?"

"I'm sorry for being a burden, a grouch, a pain in all your butts. I'm sorry for not . . . smiling. I'm sorry I didn't show my appreciation more." His voice cracked. "I'm sorry you never knew how happy I really was . . . I . . ."

He couldn't continue. Martha shushed him and squeezed his hand, then she too started to tear up. He didn't want to see her cry, so he stopped, took a breath, and looked deep into her eyes. He knew he couldn't bring any of that time back just so he could make it up to her.

"Benny, please," she whispered. "David and I, we *knew*, we *understood*. You were all *children*, and you had all experienced *so much* pain already, so *please* don't be sorry. *Please*, I beg you not to be sorry. The biggest mistake you could *ever* make is to live a life of regret. Benedict, my gift from God, my son . . ." She smiled through her tears.

His own tears fell freely when he heard those words.

"Please, *stop* looking back," she said. "Life is so short." She gulped. "David . . . David's life wasn't as long as we'd hoped, but it was full. God blessed it full of love and happiness and so many joyous moments. We couldn't have asked for more."

She held his hands. "I want that for you, Benny. I want that *so desperately* for you, but you can only have it if you stop looking back. Stop being *afraid* of what might happen, and stop regretting the things you cannot change. Only *you* have control of your happiness."

"That's what Bones said," Benedict muttered.

She laughed softly. "That's because he was a smart man." She wiped her tears away. "And his name was *Mr. Jones*, young man."

He laughed, too, and wiped his wet cheeks with his palms.

"Listen." Martha spoke carefully. "If you want me with you at Sunshine Ranch, there's no other place I'd want to be."

***

ISABELLA AND Benedict lay side by side on the wooden floor of the treehouse. The leaves of the old crooked oak rustled around them, and to Isabella it seemed as if they were all alone in the world. Through the window, she could see a sliver of moon in the black sky, but it had no authority tonight. Because Sunshine Ranch was in complete darkness, except for the string of lights that illuminated the oak and its house. It was almost as if they were floating in the darkness of the night.

She looked at Benedict, noting the grown-up traits in him, not just physically but in his sensitiveness and compassionate nature. Even so, she had no trouble seeing the child in this man. It was endearing that he had not changed in that respect. She followed his gaze over the engraved walls, remembering the exact moments that certain inscriptions were immortalized.

"*Benny is the best, Micah fails the test?*" She read and he snickered. "You were so immature, Benedict."

"Yeah, well . . . nothing's changed, y'know."

***

Isabella turned to him. "Actually, you've changed a lot, Benny." She spoke softly and he looked at her, sensing the change in her voice.

Her face was thinner than when she was a girl, and her hair was cut to her shoulders. Sometimes he forgot who she really was, but when he looked into her eyes, he found "Bella" there, and he was back home.

A gentle gust of the cool night air blew playfully through the windows above them, tapping the lantern that hung from the ceiling, and causing it to squeak and sway gently overhead. They lay watching the movement in silence, but for the sound of the lantern and the wind and the rustling. He sucked in the freshness of the air like it was a healing mist.

Isabella spoke again in an almost dreamy manner. "It was so great, wasn't it, Benny?"

"Yup."

"Are you okay?"

He watched a tiny spider crawl across the uneven ceiling. "I was just thinking about Micah."

"Micah," Isabella whispered.

Benedict told her how much he wished he'd had the opportunity to know Micah longer. She sighed and admitted that when she had tried to remember Micah, all she could remember was how much he and Benedict fought.

He groaned at that truth, because he really didn't want to be reminded of more wasted moments.

"That was all my fault," he told her. He'd been envious of Micah, and because of that, he had missed out on having a really great friend.

"Benny," she whispered. "What happened in the treehouse the day Micah died?"

23

BENEDICT STARED up at the ceiling and said, "The night Micah died, I told David that I did it. I ran away and Micah came after us, and he died because of it. David told me that I shouldn't think that way—Micah had a weak heart that had taken more than it could stand. It was like he knew more than he was telling us."

He paused as the emotions from that night returned to him. "David's heart was broken that night, Bella."

Just the thought of that incident made his nose burn and a lump rise in his throat, which he tried to swallow away.

"I had never seen a grown man cry before. He held me for a long time and then . . . he told me that only one thing could help us get through it, and he began to pray."

He could feel her watching him as he stared up into the dark, afraid to look at her.

"Oh, Benny." She touched his head.

"I've never stopped praying since that day."

They awoke in the treehouse the next morning.

"Oh, man, I think my back is broken." Benedict tried to sit up.

"Great." Isabella scratched her legs and mumbled something that ended in, "mosquito bait."

"What's the time?"

She squinted out the window. "It's time to get up. We have a lot to do today."

He was scrubbing a kitchen counter when Isabella came in carrying bags of groceries.

"Hey." She dumped the bags on the counter. "Could use your help." She marched out.

He followed her. "What did you get?"

It was promising to be a perfect day and he felt alive, as if a jolt of electricity had zapped through him—an excitement he couldn't recall ever experiencing before. He felt energized and ready to take on his future.

One of the greatest days in his life, besides arriving at Sunshine Ranch, had been the day he was adopted by David and Martha. Even after that, though, he had never been able to let go of his fears—until today. He was actually looking ahead, and soon he would be making a difference for others. At least, he hoped so.

Today was the real beginning, and he couldn't wait for the feeling of relief that would be his before the end of this day. Just the thought of it gave him butterflies.

"I picked up easy stuff." Isabella handed him some bags. "Miss Milly and her daughter are bringing the good stuff. Man, she knows how to cook. I really didn't have to talk her into it; she pretty much pushed the offer on me . . . as if I would say no. So we'll be seeing fried chicken, beans, slaw."

She followed him back to the kitchen.

"Y'know, the townspeople really miss Sunshine Ranch. It's like a part of them is gone." She stood looking at him now. "Did you ever think, as a child, that one day you'd be missed by a town? I know *I* never did."

He hadn't.

They dedicated the rest of the morning to setting up the back yard with folding chairs and picnic tables. The guests were to arrive at two o'clock, so they only had a few hours to get it all done.

"You look happy today." Isabella's eyes were narrow in accusation.

He laughed and shrugged. "Sorry."

"Don't be." She unfolded a chair and set it down. "I just have to get used to it, that's all."

He grinned and began to place the open chairs between the house and the crooked old oak. He had added more lights to the trunk of the tree the day before, and had even strung a few on some surrounding bushes. Isabella had told him not to get too carried away, but he couldn't imagine anything being over the top for this special day.

"I can't wait to see everyone." He pulled the picnic table into place. "And I *cannot* wait to bring Martha home. Wait till she sees this place."

Isabella bit her lip and said cautiously, "Benedict, are you sure you want to bring her here? I mean, she's still so upset about David and—"

"I don't care," he said. "I mean, of course I care about her, but I don't think you understand. This is Martha's home and she belongs here with her family."

"That family being you? Are you going to take care of her alone? That's a lot of responsibility."

"You know what a lot of responsibility is?" He frowned as he continued to position chairs. "Taking care of ten children that aren't your own, and doing it with more love and affection than any of our biological parents could."

As his annoyance grew, the more forceful his

movements became. "That woman was my blessing. She was there for me, and it's only right that I be there for her."

"Okay." Isabella raised her hand in surrender. "Okay, just checking." She smiled weakly.

"You know what else?" Still agitated, he just blurted it out: "I'm going to reopen Sunshine Ranch."

"Benny, are you kidding?" She collapsed onto the chair she'd just unfolded. "What do you know about raising kids?"

He sighed and sat down, as well.

"Bella, what does any parent know about raising children, until he's tried it?"

When Isabella began to protest, he told her that nothing she said would change his mind. He stood up and returned furiously to his work, while Isabella watched him with a stunned expression as he relayed how his return to Sunshine Ranch had reminded him of all the wonderful things that he got to have, on top of the amazing love that he was surrounded by, day after day. And then he asked her who he was to deprive any child of having that, if he was willing and able to provide it.

"I know the special ingredient to a happy childhood," he said in conclusion.

"You do?" She seemed amused by his confidence.

"Yes, *God*. Martha and David taught me that with God comes true happiness. 'I can do all things,' remember? Unfortunately, it took all these years for me to figure that out."

***

ISABELLA WAS SORRY that she had spoiled his mood. Even though she was impressed by the sensitive demeanor that far exceeded her initial expectation, he needed to understand the realities of his decision.

"You want to give up your life for this?"

"What life?" he asked. "Bella, I thought my life began when I grew up and left Sunshine Ranch, but the truth is that I never allowed my life to ever start."

***

The guest list had grown extensively since the invitation had been sent out. Even on short notice, a lot of people agreed to come. In addition to many of the townsfolk, Isabella had managed to contact all the Credence children. Sebastian was the first to arrive with his wife, Carla, their eight-year-old son, Micah, and five-year-old daughter, Sophia. Benedict hugged the now-tall man and they talked for the few minutes before Miss Milly and her daughter arrived with the food. Tommie arrived next as they set the food out. She was married now to Faden, who still wore cowboy hats and played the guitar. They lived close by, with their little girl, Ruth, and baby boy, Noah. And then a whole flow of people began to arrive.

Benedict's heart started to flutter against his ribcage when he realized that this was the beginning of his future. Eva arrived with her fiancé and music producer, Joe, whom she had met on tour. She was a professional singer now and she dedicated all her songs to God.

Melanie, Francine, Peachie, and Tobiah had driven in together. All in their twenties now, they lived in close proximity to each other in the city. Benedict was shocked and embarrassed to learn that Peachie actually worked near his office. He also discovered that the others had remained in close contact—it seemed he was the only one who had extracted himself from the lives of the others. Eva teased him it was because he hated them. Isabella came to his defense, but then they all pounced on her, telling her she was usually the target for his bad moods. Isabella said she didn't remember.

"I'm sorry, Bella, come here." Benedict pulled her close and squeezed her.

She pushed him away playfully. "It'll take more than that." But her eyes sparkled.

***

"Lord God, thank You for Benedict's return here to Sunshine Ranch." Fr. Thaddeus began. Standing in front of the small crowd by the lake, he looked thinner than Benedict remembered. Isabella had asked Benedict why he had chosen to drag all the guests across the field, when *she* felt that a blessing of the house would be better set by the oak tree, but he had insisted that they should see Sunshine Ranch at its best.

Fr. Thaddeus closed his eyes and raised his face toward the blue sky as he continued, his hands upraised.

"Thank You for all the goodness You have provided for the Credence children. We ask You, Lord, that You continue to bless them and their families. Bless this home and all the children who come to it. May it always be filled with love and hope and faith. Bless Benedict also, Lord, in his endeavor to save lost children, just as David and Martha saved him and Sebastian, and Eva, and Tommie, and Micah, and Isabella, and Melanie, and Francine, and Tobiah, and Peachie. And, Lord, gracious God, bless their father, David, their angel, Benjamin Jones, Nana, and their brother, Micah. Keep them close to you, Lord. They will always be in our hearts and they will always be remembered here at Sunshine Ranch. We ask this in Jesus' name, Amen."

The guests crossed themselves and smiled to each other.

"And now," Fr. Thaddeus said. "Before we proceed with the festivities, there is just one more thing Benedict asked me to do."

Benedict led the priest toward the lake, but when he reached water's edge, he didn't stop. Some of the guests gasped in surprise as Benedict and Fr. Thaddeus walked into the water.

24

MARTHA COVERED her mouth with her hands. Eva wrapped her arm around her mother's shoulder and nodded, as if she had seen it coming. Then Fr. Thaddeus spoke.

"Ladies and gentleman, yesterday your brother participated in the Solemn Rite of Baptism which, as you know includes a formal renunciation of satan and all his works, an exorcism, and anointing with Chrism. Today he stands here before you all, for the final stage of his baptism. And so it is with great pleasure that I proceed." The priest scooped water from the lake with a silver cup. "Benedict David Credence." As he poured water over Benedict's head and forehead, a tear rolled down Martha's face. "*Ego te baptizo in nomine Patris, et Filii, et Spiritus Sancti.* I baptize thee in the Name of the Father and of the Son and of the Holy Ghost."

Benedict wore a wide smile as the water ran down his face, and he raised his chin, his eyes still closed, so he could feel the sun. He thanked God for his life, and for everyone around him who cheered and yelled, "We love you, Benedict." The ache inside him finally vanished and in its place, he felt peace, and true joy.

Later, he sat with Isabella on the side of the hill overlooking Sunshine Ranch. *My home,* he thought. The guests were still mingling around, and he prayed for it to always be filled with people.

"Sunshine Ranch saved me again," he said. "That's what it does. Sunshine Ranch is supposed to be a new life for children. That's its destiny."

"Look." Isabella was gazing ahead into the sky where sun rays appeared from glowing clouds.

He followed her stare. The words, "I hear you" resounded in Benedict's mind and he smiled. *He did hear me. He always heard me. And when the time was right, He answered.*

"He knows what I'm talking about."

"I know too," Isabella said.

He looked at her as she squinted up at him. "You do?"

She nodded.

He moved a strand of hair from her face and touched her cheek with his fingers.

"Bella . . . Bella . . . Mama Bella," he said softly. "You know, you were a great mama then, what do you say?"

"What do you mean?" Her forehead wrinkled in suspicion.

He looked back at the scene by the house. "I can't do it alone. Will you help me?"

***

Isabella looked at him, perplexed. Was he asking her to work for him? It wasn't a bad idea–it's not as if she was married to her current job as a receptionist.

"Help me make Sunshine Ranch great again," he said, holding her gaze. "Be my Martha."

She was at a loss for words. Was it just help he was

looking for?

He got up and started back down the hill.

"Benny." She rushed after him. *"Benny!"* As she got closer, he turned to her and she bumped into him before she could stop.

"Is that a yes?" His eyebrows rose in question.

Was he playing with her? She was still getting used to this new Benedict; this compassionate Benedict, whose sole purpose in life now seemed to be making other children happy. *What is he asking me?*

***

"YOUR FAMILY is amazing, Sabe. *You* are a lucky man."

Benedict was sitting with Sebastian in the entranceway of the treehouse, now lit with Christmas lights, while the party continued below at a slower pace.

"Lucky? Yes. I truly am." They both looked down at Carla.

"What about your father?" he asked.

"Oh, man." Sebastian smiled. "He is a changed man. It's amazing. Well, not really changed, but he's back to the way he was before my mother died, y'know? He even remarried."

"Really?"

"Yup, and his wife is really great. She's not Mom, and she's far from Martha, but she's pretty nice, and she and my father are happy."

"That's great."

"Yeah . . . and they *love* the kids," Sebastian said. "They are so involved in their lives. It's so good for kids to have grandparents. Carla's parents are great, too. And Martha . . . any child who has Martha is a *lucky* kid."

They watched Martha now as she laughed with Eva,

215

Tommie, little Micah, and Sophia.

"I just wish . . ." Sebastian pressed his lips tightly together.

"I know," Benedict said. "I wish it too."

"It's really amazing how life turns out, don't you think?" He paused and then asked, "What about you?"

"What about me?"

"You're not getting any younger. Do you have a special someone back home that you'll be bringing back here?"

"Nope, I think I have everything I need right here." He looked down at Isabella now, who was covering baby Noah with kisses, until he began to cry.

"It's okay." Tommie giggled. "He needs a change."

"Oh, do you need me to. . . ."

"Uh, no." Tommie laughed. "I've got this."

"Old habits die hard." Isabella kissed Tommie as she handed the baby over. She looked around her, and then up at Benedict.

Sebastian followed Benedict's stare. "Bella never let any of us go. I'm not just talking about visiting us when we were kids. Even after we all left, she kept in touch. She always did have a way of taking care of everyone. She kept us all together."

"Yes, she did."

"Well, I need to hit the men's room." Standing on the ladder, he stopped and faced Benedict. "Thanks for letting us stay here tonight."

"Are you kidding? We're family, Sabe." Benedict looked at him sincerely. "You're always welcome. I hope you visit more and visit often."

"Hey, you'll never get rid of us."

"I hope not." They hugged before Sebastian descended the ladder, where he met Isabella at the bottom. He kissed her on the forehead.

She climbed up toward Benedict and stood on the ladder in front of him.

"I made baby Noah cry," she said seriously.

"You did?"

"Yes, I did."

"That wasn't very nice."

"No, it wasn't. Are you sure you want me to help you here?"

He moved aside so she could sit next to him.

"Only if you want to."

They both looked down at their family enjoying the evening. Martha and Peachie were now sitting with Sophia, while Melanie fussed over her. Carla, Eva, and Tommie were sharing humorous stories about their children. Faden was playing his guitar, as little Micah watched intently, his uncle's cowboy hat on his head. Fr. Thaddeus sat close by with little Noah in his arms sucking on a bottle of warm milk, rocking him to the music. Tobiah, Francine, and Joe entertained Ruth. It was a wonderful sight.

Isabella reached for Benedict's hand.

"I want to," she said.

"Good. Now you know what would make this evening pretty much perfect?"

"What?" She whispered her question.

He leaned toward her and she gasped softly. Then he whispered into her ear, "A slice of Miss Milly's lemon meringue pie." He pulled back, signaling to the ladder. "Go on, you first."

She bit her lip, and he noticed her eyes glisten as she started to descend.

"Hey," he said softly.

When she looked up at him, he leaned in toward her, and this time he pressed a soft kiss on her lips.

"Look at that." Eva pointed to Benedict and Isabella at

the top of the ladder.

"Oh, my," Carla said.

"Gross," Tommie said.

Eva clasped her hands together in front of her chin. "That's so great."

"Who'd a guessed it," Tommie said. "Benny and Bella sitting in a tree, K.I.S.S.I.N.G. . . ."

END

Other titles by T.M. Gaouette you may enjoy:

Faith & Kung Fu Series:
Freeing Tanner Rose- Book 1
Saving Faith -Book 2

Made in the USA
Coppell, TX
21 August 2020

33843359R00132